A Chance to Tell Ten Stories

Stanley B. Trice

This book is a work of fiction. Names, characters, places, and incidents are the product of the author's imagination or used fictitiously. Any resemblance to actual events, places, or persons is coincidental.

Copyright © 2022 by Stanley B. Trice
Published by Every Word Rise, LLC
Place of Publication: New Bern, NC

Cover and interior design by Woven Red Author Services, www.WovenRed.ca

All rights reserved. No part of this publication may be stored in a retrieval system, reproduced, or transmitted by any means electronic, mechanical, photocopying, recording, or otherwise without prior written permission from the author.

Library of Congress Control Number: 2022901107

ISBN for Print: 978-0-9909265-5-9
ISBN for Ebook:978-0-9909265-6-6

Other Books by Stanley B. Trice

High School Rocket Science (For Extraterrestrial Use Only)

Evidence of a Commuter Train

Contents

Sisters

I once worked with a woman who had a younger sister. The woman told me how she and her sister did not get along until they went to their grandfather's funeral. They both always competed for his attention and standing in front of his coffin, they decided he wasn't worth it. They became sisters and friends.

Looking out the passenger side window, Beth watched streaks of drizzling rain blur the passing farmland. In the distance, gray clouds hung low, causing her ghostly reflection in the glass. Beside her, David drove in silence with his clean-shaven face losing its summer tan. As usual, his blond hair needed a comb. Nevertheless, her husband was striking in his dark blue suit.

"This is going to be one dreary day. I hope this doesn't take too long," he said, finally. "I've got a lot of work to do at the office."

"This is my grandpa's funeral. Couldn't you be a little more considerate of my feelings?" Beth said, clenching her teeth.

She used to tolerate David's workaholic attitude. Now, his overzealous, competitive desire toward his work made her wish he was seeing another woman. Then I'd know how to fight back, she thought. Swelling tenseness narrowed her oval eyes and creased her forehead. She swiped a locket of limp black hair away from her high cheekbones.

"I'm not being inconsiderate. I just made a statement I think both of us can agree on."

"You always have a lot of work to do and *yes* you are being inconsiderate. This funeral isn't going to be pleasant for me."

Beth stared at the passing farmland. She remembered the horseback rides years ago through the same rolling countryside with her grandpa, her mother's father. They would ride under the arching reach of stout elms and follow white washed fences to gated ends. Back then, Grandpa's thick white hair tousled in the wind while her pigtails spiked the air as she rode quick to keep up. He was always younger than his body, Beth thought.

Tears swelled in her eyes and regret flooded Beth as she thought about the waning contact that seeped between them over the years. The laughter associated with the time of horseback rides was distant.

After a few more minutes of silence, David blurted out, "I don't care. We're leaving right after the funeral. I've got to get back to my office."

Beth knew too much about David. She could picture his thoughts racing about his job. "You're obsessed with getting that director's position," she said.

"If you would listen to me sometimes you'd know that selection is in two weeks and I'm not the only competitor for it." David clicked his tongue, which he did when irritated. "I need to work on my marketing presentation. It could determine who gets the position."

"You already told me that rumor has you in the lead. Can't you think about other things for a change?" Lately, Beth found herself challenging David's attitude about his job more and more.

"I'm not going to explain it to you again. All I'm asking is that we not waste time after the funeral," he said.

"Look, David. We can't just leave like that." Beth snapped her fingers, releasing a small explosion of anger. "Your precious work can wait. This is my grandpa and my family. I know that doesn't mean much to you, but it does to me."

"All right." David said. He paused. "I've never liked funerals, anyway. They creep me out. Besides, you haven't seen your grandfather in years."

"Yes, since we've been married," Beth said. His last statement hurt. A card here and there to his grandpa and an occasional call was not enough.

"Besides, I don't see any need for me to hang around with your family. I hardly knew your grandfather. You are going to tell them today, aren't you? It'll be a good opportunity with everyone there."

"Don't be absurd. I can't tell them at my grandpa's funeral. And could you please not mention anything? I can't deal with more than one crisis at a time," Beth said. Their visits to separate lawyers and David's plans to move out in a few days tormented her.

"All right, all right. But you'll have to tell your family soon."

"I know, but not right now." Beth wanted the argument to end.

She could manage her dad, telling him about her failed marriage. But Beth didn't know how she was going to tell her mother. David and Beth turned their attention toward their own thoughts and rode the rest of the way in silence. Only the sound of the car slicing through the rain was heard between them.

Arriving at the farmhouse, David maneuvered around several cars cluttered along the gravel driveway. On their way to the long wooden front porch, Beth and David warded off misting rain with separate umbrellas. The well-lit house inside defied the shadowy weather outside.

Most of the men grouped in the living room near the wet bar where David went. Beth smiled at her dad as he stood tall among the men. Except his smile and attention were with David, who approached. Beth kept walking.

Most of the women milled around the dining room table in an adjacent room. Beth didn't see her younger sister Annette, her mother, or Grandma among them. Respectfully, she chatted with her aunts and cousins before wandering into the kitchen.

"Beth, I'm glad you're here," Grandma said, sitting at the kitchen table. She smiled softly at Beth as if glad she had come.

"Grandma, I'm so sorry," Beth said, bending over and hugging the aged woman.

Grandma had a youthful plumpness to her features and strength to her grip. Her long gray hair was pulled back in a bun as usual.

Mother sat across the table in her authoritative pose with her black dress pressed exactly so. Seated next to her was Annette, who matched Mother in facial features. Annette's long, ashen hair was neatly combed and pinned back. Her dark burgundy dress had a slight print of flower petals along the collar and hem that highlighted her large brown eyes. Beth felt guilty about the plain dark emerald green dress she wore. She felt sloppy and out of color.

"It's too bad you couldn't be at the viewing last night," Mother said. "Dad looked wonderful. But at least Annette made it."

"I'm sure Beth couldn't help not being at the viewing, Mom," said Annette. "I live a lot closer and Beth would have been there if she could."

"I did try to come," Beth said, angry at her mother's comments and puzzled by Annette's defense.

"Anyway, I'm glad you're here today," Grandma said. "It's good so many people came. John would have been pleased."

"Why don't we go in the dining room," suggested Mother. "Other guests have probably arrived."

With Mother leading, Annette passed close to Beth and whispered, "Don't pay any attention to Mom. She's upset about Grandpa's death. Besides, you know Mom has to have everything perfect."

"Yeah, but she's right. I should have been at the viewing last night." Beth angrily remembered how David came home late, so they missed the viewing. She could have gone alone, except she would have had to answer questions from Mother over David's absence.

The two younger women followed the two older ones into the quiet conversations in the house. Beth allowed the swarm of relatives to envelop and hide her. Serious comments were avoided.

When the time came to leave for the funeral, Mother insisted that fewer cars be used and people ride together. Beth pressed for her and David to ride alone. She did not want to be trapped in a discussion about herself, David, and their future. Mostly, she wanted to be alone and she knew she would be that way with David. In the end, it was Dad winning the argument for Beth that irritated Mother.

The funeral home was in a converted house. Where it once had life, now it hosted the remains of life. At the front of a long room, a dark mahogany casket sat on a metal pedestal with short wooden benches facing the casket in a bad attempt at order. The intent was to encourage a good view of the coffin, but prevented talk between attendees.

Beth sat on a hard bench between Dad and David while in front of them Annette sat between her husband Rick and Mother. The two women held hands and clutched tissues together. Beth sat clutching her own tissues as the two men beside her paid attention to the quality of the casket.

A tall thin preacher in a tight fitting black suit gave a cordial ceremony where his words made the audience quiet. He spoke of Grandpa's boyish enjoyment of life, causing Beth to think of so many memories at one time she couldn't focus on a single one. She tried to hold back tears, yet she ended up patting them away with a single torn tissue. She sat between her two men, who did not hold her hands.

From the funeral home, the cars formed a procession and drove through the small town toward open farmland. Five miles out, the line of vehicles passed through wrought-iron gates and into a land of granite and marble monuments nestled among a spread of old hardwood trees. The rain had subsided, but gray clouds hung threateningly low.

On a bright day, it could be peaceful here, Beth thought. More people arrived to crowd around the canopy and casket and listen to the final words of the preacher.

As he spoke, Beth let her thoughts drift away to when she was ten-years-old. She remembered a walk with Dad and Grandpa, each gently holding her hands. The three strolled along a well-worn cow path, across pastured lands, and between rounded hillsides surveying the farm. The men she was descended from talked in deep tones with words that did not matter to her. It was their voices that were a comfort, like the soft blow of wind high in the trees.

The memory gave way to thoughts about her wedding when she passed from one man's hands to another. Beth realized that this time when she passes out of marriage no one will be there to hold her hand. Somehow, knowing this gave her a growth of confidence. She could feel herself get stronger and happier, accepting that she could hold her own hands if she wanted.

Walking away after the funeral, Annette asked Beth, "You're coming back to the house, aren't you?"

"Yes, for a little while." Beth sensed urgency in her sister's voice and suddenly David's wants irritated her. "If David wants to leave early, I can stay and catch a ride from someone else."

"That'll be great. I'll see you at the house," Annette said as she quickly caught up to her husband Rick.

On the way back, Beth told David, "Annette wants me to stay awhile. So, if you're in a hurry to leave, go ahead. I'll find a way back."

"I hope you'll find time to tell them about our divorce."

"I'll tell my family, but right after Grandpa's funeral is not the time." Beth felt tears swell in her eyes, yet she contained them.

"Okay, tell them whenever you want. They're your family. I'll wait around a little while at the house."

Beth rolled down the window to let the cool, damp air contain her emotions. The rain started again and she let the water dampen her hair and steal down her neckline and back. Still, her burdens did not lift and too soon she rolled up the window.

At the farmhouse, Beth walked alone, leaving David behind. He could have been like one of the nearby trees or a cloud passing overhead. Invisible to her. In the house, there was no opportunity to speak to Grandma because Mother flanked her protectively. Beth talked to her dad, but it was not the same as she remembered.

A hug from him made her feel like a small girl and she was not sure she liked the fatherly protection. David came over and stole the respect Beth desired from her dad. She did not want to stay in the presence of the two men.

Beth accepted that she had drifted away from her tomboy self to a different person. Womanhood signified not only growing up, but moving courageously on. She would reacquaint herself with her dad at another time in another frame of mind, she thought, while walking away.

Beth felt drawn to the women of the family she knew little about. But she needed to find her sister first. Annette was alone in a back bedroom, sitting on the bed and staring out a pane glass window and the gray weather.

"Annette, why are you sitting here by yourself?" Beth asked.

"I needed some time alone," she replied. "It was a nice funeral, wasn't it?"

Beth sat on the bed beside her sister. "Yeah, but I wish I had seen Grandpa more these last few years."

"I was always jealous of you and Grandpa when we were kids. But that was how it worked out. You with Grandpa and me with Grandma." The words came suddenly from Annette with a tone of resentment.

"I'm sorry you felt like that."

"I didn't mean it to sound hateful. I just don't want it to always be that way between us." Turning to Beth, Annette continued, "I need to tell you something."

"What is it?" Outside the room, Beth heard people leaving. She wondered if David was among them.

Annette turned her gaze back toward the window. "I'm afraid Rick is seeing another woman."

"How do you know?"

"I was suspicious for a while because of a strange perfume on him and when I called him at work, he wouldn't be there. Then, I found a note in his pocket from someone named Suzie."

The tears came then and Beth held her younger sister. After a few moments, Annette drew away, saying, "I'm sorry. I really don't know what to do."

"You'll have to decide what's best for you and tell him you know."

"What if he wants to be with her?"

"It's better to find out now than later." Beth wanted to instill hope in her sister. How can I do that when my own marriage is over?

"If Rick and I split, Mom will be angry. She's put so much pressure on me for my marriage to succeed and for me to have children."

Mother would eventually accept my failed, childless marriage, but not Annette's, Beth thought. Dad would be my problem, yet he will not put the pressure on me that Mother will put on Annette.

"Forget, Mom. She's not married to Rick and you are. Do you want Rick back?"

"I don't know anymore."

It grew lighter outside as the clouds cleared. Beth reached for her sister's hand, both unable to talk. They sat together on the bed listening to the house empty of parents, husbands, and family. Through the window they watched the sun break through the clouds and fill the bedroom with brightness.

Harboring a Change

I read a memoir of a man who, at forty years old, had a sex change operation (now called sex reassignment). He had two grown children and a wife and the memoir was more about them and how they were coping then what he was experiencing, physically and emotionally.

As he approached his fortieth birthday, Papa announced in an email the upcoming date of his sex change operation. He had finished his year of hormone replacement and wanted the operation like a birthday present to himself.

Until the email, my twin sister Sue and me, her twin brother, knew nothing about Papa's desire to change himself. In his email, he went on explaining how he always wanted to be a woman. *Now is the time before I get too old,* Papa wrote. *I have never been happy as a man. I thought if I changed sex, I would be happy. Happy people live longer. I want to live.*

I was confused. I thought he was going through some mid-life crisis. But someone like that usually goes on a trip to somewhere they may not survive or they buy something too expensive for them to afford. After reading his email again and again, I was still confused. Papa had never shown any desire to be a woman.

However, I could see him keeping a secret like this. Papa was always a private person, which Mom didn't seem to mind. She was outgoing enough for the two of them.

Mom was also on the "To" line and my sister and I soon learned, through a series of "replies" from her, that this was how Mom found out her husband wanted to be a woman.

I thought Mom should have been the least surprised by Papa's decision. She lived with him. Didn't she notice the changes to his body from the hormone replacement he took for a year? That this operation was a surprise to her showed what their relationship was after twenty years of marriage.

Sue and I did notice Papa's extra body fat and changes in his face. But being twenty year olds, we thought that's what happens when men reach forty.

An hour after the email, my mother called to tell me about the divorce, that Papa would be moving out, and her opinion of Papa's decision.

"He's a pervert." She shrieked into my smartphone, which was not smart enough to keep her voice from banging off my ear and splashing across my one-bedroom apartment.

"A year ago, your father moved into the spare bedroom in the basement. I thought nothing of it. I was happy to be alone with my wine, book club, and hot flashes. When I saw him, I just thought he was getting fat. Anyway, he was always wearing those bulky clothes, so it was hard to tell."

I hoped to calm my mother by resorting to science, my fallback option.

"Technically, it's called sex reassignment surgery, and Papa can't actually change his sex. All he can do is alter his physical appearance to come as close as possible to the anatomy of a woman," I said.

"Your medical explanation don't explain why he's doing this. He's forty years old, damn it, and before his email he never talked to me about this decision of his."

"What would you have done if he had told you?"

"I would have told him he was being a pervert."

"Hold on, I got another call."

"Sam, this is Sue. You read Papa's email? My god, he's going through so much and Mom isn't even supporting him. Doesn't she know that he's just realigning his body to be who he felt he always was. Mom doesn't understand that dad is making things right with himself," she said.

"I agree with you. But Mom is against this."

"Maybe she'd be alright with his operation if she knew he's not having his penis cut off. It's just being inverted inside of him so he can have vaginal lips," said Sue.

"I don't think telling her that will help. Hold on, I got another call," I said. I didn't want to hear any more details about Papa's operation. Particularly when it dealt with a body part I had.

"Mom, where is Papa staying..."

"You're a man. What's going on here? Do all men want to be women? Believe me, it's not all that easy."

I thought if she got any louder I would need hearing aids. I didn't dare ask when my parents last had sex. Obviously, not in the past year.

"Maybe this is something he's always wanted," I said.

"What's wrong with you? You're my son and you need to be on my side. I know Sue is already siding with *him*."

"Hold on, I got another call." I didn't know we were picking sides. "Are you sure Papa's doing the right thing, Sue?"

"He's got a lot of courage to do this. I wish I could be half as brave as he is."

"When Papa has his surgery, he'll need help being a woman," I said.

"I'm not helping him with any of this. That's disgusting."

I didn't know whether or not I switched calls. I didn't know who I was talking to or what I just said. Mom and Sue's voices sounded too much alike.

"Who are you talking to on the other line?"

I wondered who asked the question.

"This is your mother. You just go ahead and side with Sue."

I switched calls since there was only one left.

"Sue..."

"You were talking to Mom, weren't you? Well, just go ahead and side with her."

I stood in my living room, that was also my kitchen and partly my bedroom, not wanting to be on anyone's side. Since I got along with Sue a lot more, being basically the male version of her, I went to her apartment. It was a lot bigger than mine.

When Sue opened the door, I asked, "You're a woman. Why does Papa want to do this?"

"Being a woman does not explain why a man wants to be one," Sue said, spinning back into her apartment.

I followed her. "I read from the hospital website that he'll be in post-op for eight days. He'll have some pain, but not as much as people expect." I decided not to go into details of creating a vagina, since Sue had one and had already explained it to me.

"I guess he'll be tired a lot afterwards." Sue got busy making herself a sandwich.

"He'll be on a catheter for the first four days. I think he'll need an enema to get everything working again," I said.

"Go on. I figured that would happen."

"After eight days, the hospital will discharge him. He should be back at work at the accounting firm in about three weeks." I didn't mention that Papa could have sex with a man or a woman about six weeks after surgery.

"I'm assuming Mom won't help," Sue said.

"They're getting a divorce."

"They don't need to divorce. Same sex couples can be married in this state," said Sue.

I stared at my sister making her sandwich and wondered if she really understood what was happening. "I don't think Mom wants to be married to another woman who used to be her husband."

She was making a bologna and cheese sandwich. "Yeah, alright."

Sue took a big bite of her sandwich and, with her mouth full, said, "You take care of him while he's in the hospital. On the eighth day when he's discharged he'll be a she and I'll take over. Deal?" She took another chomp on her sandwich.

"Okay." I said. I wondered who would take care of Mom.

Papa died on his seventh day in the hospital. He had been doing so well up to that point that the nurses unplugged electronic instruments from his body surfaces. With all the attention on Papa's lower half, the doctors missed the minor heart infraction deep in his left ventricle.

Mom insisted on a funeral and Sue wanted a cremation. I wanted Papa to be alive, so they left me out of the decision making. Since storing Papa's body was getting expensive, they finally agreed on a funeral first and cremation second.

At the funeral, the family patriarch lay in a polished mahogany box in a dark blue suit looking like a mannequin. With worn carpeting and faded walls, the shabby funeral home looked like it should have a funeral for itself.

"We should have put him in a dress," said Sue.

"I don't want people remembering him as a woman," Mom said. "We'll burn him in a dress. He can be whatever he wants when he's a pile of ashes."

I thought Mom was being more accepting of Papa's decision now that he was dead.

After the funeral and cremation, Sue and I left Mom and went to the reception in the house we grew up in. We kept moving through the rooms, avoiding the collected breaths of relatives we saw during weddings and funerals. But we couldn't avoid Mom. She danced around a tour of talkative relatives and planted herself in front of us.

"You left the funeral home before I could tell you. I'm beach bound," she announced.

I heard relatives nearby munching on cheesy crackers like an out of tune orchestra. All I could think of was Papa being a pile of ashes while people stuffed their faces with our cheap food.

"What's at the beach that's not here?" Sue threw her paper plate across the nearest table of food.

"My sister Anna. I convinced her to co-buy a cottage on the beach. We're all that's left on my side of the family."

Sue and I heard laughter erupt down the narrow hallway. Mom stepped closer to us so we could hear better.

"Your father inherited this house from his father, who got it from his father. I don't intend to continue the legacy. I'm having an auction next Saturday. In the meantime, take whatever you want. I'll sell what's left at the auction."

Mom disappeared toward the laughter, leaving us children holding glasses of sweet punch, dirty napkins, and broken crackers.

Before the auction, my sister and I scanned the stuff left over from our childhood and took nothing. Mom said nothing. There was nothing to be said to end our lives together as a family. Except, I could not let the house go to a stranger.

It took all my savings and future savings to outbid two house flippers who would have turned the house into mini-condos and no longer a house I grew up in. Mom kept silent as she took my money, leaving me with the biggest debt I ever had.

A month later with summer heat strong, Anna called to tell me that a rip current had carried Mom away from the shoreline. She drowned in the ocean depths she always wanted to live near. My Aunt Anna told me this the same day she had Mom cremated. I got her ashes and Aunt Anna kept Mom's money, most of which used to be mine.

"I wish I was as brave as Papa for taking a chance to be happy," Sue said. We sat at the kitchen table cradling cups of hot tea between our palms. We had just finished dumping our mother's ashes in the front flower bed. She had dumped Papa's ashes there saying he would make excellent fertilizer. We followed our mother's advice.

"I think Papa killed himself," I said.

"Bravery and suicide can be the same thing when you're someone you're not." Sue said, sipping her hot tea carefully with loud slurps.

"I don't know what that means."

"He took a chance knowing he might die," Sue said, staring into her tea. "Why don't you have cookies around here that I can have with my tea?"

Sue went home a short time later. She wanted a nap before meeting with her friends later. I didn't want to be around people. Instead, I walked around the house doing that inventory of furnishings I promised Sue I would do. Just in case I needed to sell things to keep the place from falling down. Later that night, the police called.

The voice coming out of my smartphone sounded tired. I was tired. But I listened to a person I would never talk to again explain that Sue had been in an accident.

At the hospital, medical people were administrative and formal, not sympathetic and understanding. They would not take the time to explain the accident or her death. Instead, they handed me a stack of papers to sign so I could claim her body.

I sat alone outside a clerical office in a sterile corridor reading that Sue was hit by a bus. Probably the one she was running to catch since she was always late trying to catch it. I looked around the empty corridor, thinking I heard her voice. Although I missed her terribly, I hoped she didn't stick around to haunt me.

I went home and fell into bed listening to the house creak and trying not to think how all my family was dead. Eventually I fell asleep and had a wild ass dream with Sue standing at the foot of my bed in what looked like meringue pie.

"You're dead," I said to her in my dream.

"Getting hit by that bus didn't hurt, but that damn ambulance ride did," said Sue. She looked like herself, except transparent and hazy and ghost-like.

"Are you supposed to say 'damn' when you're dead?" I wondered whether this was a dream, a nightmare, or I was awake and wishing I was dreaming and not having a nightmare.

Some loud creak in the house woke me up as if the place was ready to fall down. Ghostly Sue continued to stand, or maybe float, at the foot of my bed.

"Good, now you're awake. I can talk better like this," she said.

"I don't want you to be dead. I want you to be alive. What am I going to do now?" The grief was sweeping over me like sheets of rain. Finally, the feeling left as if the sun came out.

"Is that better? I got most of the grief out of you in one swoop," said Ghostly Sue, waving her arm through the air like she was trying to fly.

"I want to die and be with you."

"You'll die, but not for some time. How 'bout I stick around until you find someone to love. You always struggled with love. Now that I am who I am I can help," said Sue.

She haunted me until I sold the old house a month later to Aunt Anna, who wanted to get away from the constant roar of the ocean. My aunt claimed it was my mother's idea to live by the sea. Besides, I didn't have the money to keep the house from coming down on me, even if I sold the contents.

Aunt Anna paid for the house with money I paid to buy the house and I almost broke even in the exchange. She kept the extra money to make repairs. I moved back into Sue's apartment, since it was bigger than mine. I also went to Aunt Anna's open house party.

Walking among the same relatives from Papa's funeral, I missed Sue. She had not been haunting me since I moved into her apartment and I found myself wishing for happiness like Papa. I went back to the apartment and, after a year on hormone replacement, had the sex reassignment operation Papa died from.

"What did you do that for?" Sue came back by sending a crack down the middle of the full-length mirror I stood naked in front of.

New medical procedures created a better vagina than Papa's. Even my hips were wider. Also, my breasts had real alveoli cavities and lobules for more feeling in my wide, red nipples. My boobs were bigger than Sue's and the crack was sent in revenge.

I wrapped my new body in a cotton bathrobe to keep her from breaking anything else.

"What is it with all the men of this family wanting to be women? You know, it doesn't matter when you're dead. There are no sexes around here."

"Living as a man wasn't working out for me."

"You thought the change would kill you like it did Papa. I'm a ghost. I know these things."

"Where have you been, anyway?"

"Time is irrelevant around here. I thought it had only been a few hours. I guess I missed Aunt Anna's party."

"Yeah, and everything else that happened to me in the past year."

"Hey, there's a lot to learn about haunting."

"I didn't like being alone. I want to go with you."

I threw open the robe in front of the cracked mirror that made my body look like two distorted images. "Look at this. Medical procedures have gotten too good and now I have this female body."

"You do have a damn good looking body for a woman," Sue said through the crack in the mirror. Her face became my left breast.

"So here I am a woman when I want to be dead." I didn't tell her how I liked my new body.

"How 'bout I stick around for another year. If you still feel glummy, I'll see what I can do to kill you."

I was happy with this lie.

Sue helped me find Jerry, who used to be a woman. We married and moved in with Aunt Anna. She was lonely in the old house and wanted our company. She helped us adopt a two-year-old girl claiming to be reincarnated from a man who died after wanting to be a woman.

Halloween Ugly

I once volunteered to be president of a small homeowners association after no one would take the job. This story is so much like my experiences as president and I quickly learned why no one else volunteered.

"Jeff, hold the ladder steady," Harris said.

"You forget I'm blind. I can't see whether the ladder is steady or not."

"You can feel the ladder moving. You can hear me telling you to hold the ladder steady," said Harris as he struggled to fix a light on the entrance sign to Majestic Avenue. It was the single road in and out of Trailer Paradise where the half mile long line of single wides, long end in, sat on each side like soldiers standing guard.

"If you get off the ladder, I can hold it better," said Jeff.

"I'll get off the ladder as soon as I put in this new light bulb."

Harris wished he had other board members on the Trailer Paradise Association to help. Except one moved away to get off the board and the other bought a whip to keep people from bothering him. Harris climbed down the ladder and found Jeff leaning against the sign's metal post instead of holding the ladder.

"Being blind doesn't give you an excuse to let go of the ladder," said Harris. "I could have fallen."

"I held it until my arms got tired. Besides, what if you fell? It'd be an improvement in your looks."

"How do you know what I look like? You can't see me."

"I hear people talk. I believe them just like I believe an extra-terrestrial is renting one of the trailers."

"Believe whatever you want. I don't care. I want to fix one more thing before we quit for the afternoon," said Harris.

He tried not to think about what people said about him. His whole life, people talked about how he looked and he tried to ignore them like he tried to ignore that he was ugly.

"Let's quit now. If people cared about things around here, they'd be helping you and I'd be home resting," said Jeff.

"People care, they're just busy."

"I'm busy and I'm out here helping you," said Jeff.

"I don't want to talk about this anymore. Besides, this fix won't take long. It's that light on one of the two brick pillars where the avenue meets the main road."

"You mean those tall brick pillars? The ones no one ever looks at? Besides, I never understood why we have two entrances thirty feet apart."

"I don't know why we have two entrances, but you never look at them 'cause you're blind. Now, come with me. The Vice President, a.k.a. you, is supposed to help the President, i.e. me."

"As I've said before, I never accepted no nomination for VP."

"Should've come to the meeting last week when I nominated you. It was a unanimous decision since no one else wanted the job."

"I don't think that's how board elections work." Jeff remained leaning against the pole. "It doesn't matter now. You're my VP, so let's go." Harris grabbed Jeff's thrift store coat with one hand while dragging the aluminum ladder with the other.

Jeff's coat felt like tweed and it reminded Harris when he was twelve-years-old. He followed his father then, who wore a tweed jacket, as they walked up to the orphanage. At that time, it had been two years after his mother died from cancer.

In the tall foyer of the orphanage, his father smelled of liquor, like he usually did, and mumbled to Harris about missing his wife too much to take care of his son anymore. The last thing Harris saw was his father walking away with his tweed jacket thrown over his sagging shoulder.

Six years later, when Harris left the orphanage for community college, his discharge papers included a letter from his father. The scrawl hoped Harris had a better life with someone else. In the six years at the orphanage, Harris learned that his looks would not give him a better life with someone else. He had a better life before the orphanage.

Harris crowded these memories out of his head as he finished towing Jeff and the ladder to the brick pillar. Pulling his wool jacket closer to his body, the thick hair on his chest and backside pushed back. He wished he could afford a good quality tweed coat to do a better job at hiding his ugly, hairy body.

Except the tweed would not hide his bulky face with the hanging nose, unbalanced cheeks, and twisted chin. With his drooping eyes, what he saw in the mirror each morning was an image people did not look at for long. He wished his mom had lived, then his parents could have helped him in life with his looks.

"Crap, Harris. This pillar feels too tall," said Jeff, who felt the coarse bricks as high as he could reach.

"The ladder may be a little short, but it'll work if you hold it this time."

Harris wedged the ladder against the rough pillar bricks, placed Jeff's hands on the metal rungs, and climbed until reaching the top step labeled "Do Not Stand." Struggling to reach higher, Harris wrapped his thick right arm around the tarnished brass lantern. Balanced this way, he hunted in his coat for pliers to take out the rusted wing nuts. Not finding the tool, he remembered the tool was in his new single wide trailer.

A month ago, just before Halloween, Harris moved from his used single wide at the back end of Majestic Avenue into his renovated and extra-long single wide at the beginning of the Avenue. His address stayed Trailer Paradise, yet he was that much closer to the entrance and leaving. It was one of those things making Harris feel as if he was making progress in his life.

"Jeff, you got pliers on you?"

"Harris, all I got is this ladder."

Both turned quickly toward squealing tires and grinding gears, both moaning viciously toward the brick pillars.

"Run!" Harris yelled.

He should have climbed down the ladder before telling Jeff to run. The ladder teetered and fell, leaving Harris scrambling toward the top of the brick pillar. He desperately clutched at the tarnished lantern.

Pulling himself higher, Harris spied a burgundy, two-door sedan miss the easy turn off the main road. The car jumped the shallow drainage ditch and plowed sideways into the brick pillar below him. The muffled sound of crushing metal sent a puff of excited steam and oil smells into the humid air.

From a distance, Jeff yelled, "Hey, Harris. You alright? I don't want to be promoted to president."

"Yeah, I'm fine. A car side-swiped the pillar. Come help the driver."

Harris peered down at the dull roof and recognized it as the widow Mrs. Filbert's car. She demanded people use "Mrs." as a tribute to her wealthy husband, whose fortune she lost on scratch-offs and lottery games. The eighty-three-year-old woman with cataracts who walked with a cane on one side and a crutch on the other had run over quite a lot lately.

"You okay, Mrs. Filbert?" Harris hoped her car was unfixable.

"Shut up, you damn ugly president." Her head stuck out of the car's open window, looking like a white-haired, bobble head. "If you'd fixed that damn light, I'd seen what damn thing I hit."

"Hey, Mrs. Filbert," said Jeff.

"Shut up, you damn blind ass. I'm gonna sue this damn homeowner's board for having damn freaks working on it. I never went to no damn meeting, and I never elected no damn fool board members like you two damn freaks. I'm gonna sue, damn you!"

Harris learned long ago not to argue with her. She had nurtured and groomed, for too many years, an unreal and unfactual opinion about reality. Harris jumped on top of the hood and to the ground, figuring another dent in the car would not matter. He helped Jeff pull open Mrs. Filbert's stuck car door.

Jeff, being blind, caught Mrs. Filbert's crutch in his chest. Harris managed to avoid the swinging cane. Jeff was on his own getting off the ground.

"I need help getting to my damn house. Which one of you damn fools is taking me? If you don't, I'll sue."

"I'll take you," Jeff said. "Harris don't need me to hold him up to the light no more. He's got something to stand on now."

"Well, get your damn ass over here and start helping me, you damn blind fool. I ain't got all damn night. My damn *Wheel of Fortune* is comin' on soon and if I miss that damn show I'll sue, damn you."

Harris watched the two of them stumble up Majestic Avenue and into the heart of Trailer Paradise. Jeff's teasing and Mrs. Filbert's cussing would surely draw complaints from the neighbors. Harris turned off his smartphone so he wouldn't get the calls. Suddenly, fat raindrops struck the top of his head.

Harris hated rain because it made him sweat more. He climbed into Mrs. Filbert's car and pulled the door closed as the rain came fatter and faster. He was glad the car was old enough to have roll-up windows.

Sitting there listening to the rain, Harris remembered two weeks ago it was supposed to rain on Halloween night, but didn't. He wished it had. The trailer park had a reputation for safely giving out a lot of candy and treats and too many children came for other neighborhoods. Being at the back of Majestic Avenue, he usually had few trick-or-treaters. Being at the front, he had all of them. Particularly after word got out among the parents that he was dressed as a costumed horror figure. Harris wished he had been dressed like that and not wearing his normal clothes.

Inside the car, he listened to the rain pound the metal roof and wondered what style of tweed his father would have liked most. Herringbone, barleycorn, houndstooth, or just plain twill tweed? He sat alone in the musty car, letting his sweaty ugliness become like an old friend.

Through the rain-soaked windshield, Harris spied the groundhog Potter near the other brick pillar. Barely holding its round belly off the road from too many people feeding it, the furry animal waddled into Trailer Paradise. Probably looking for its burrow, Harris concluded. Never seeing Potter with other groundhogs, Harris wondered if it had a family. There were enough lonely people in Trailer Paradise.

The rain beat harder on the car and Harris remembered a few years ago his attempt at dating.

The first two women he dated ended quickly. The third woman demanded to see his bank statement. There was not enough money for her to stay. Harris stopped trying and became the association president to meet people. Except, the only person he met was Jeff, who was blind. He ignored Jeff's suggestion that Harris date women who were blind.

Listening to the rain, Harris pictured himself in his new single wide and sitting in his new red leather recliner that he bought as a housewarming gift to himself. The delivery men put it in the middle of his living room and left the plastic on, so Harris left it on, too. There was no room for any other furniture and the plastic helped Harris believe he would one day move to a house that could not be easily towed away.

His new recliner faced his new large screen TV that filled the entire wall of his living room. With his renovated single wide, red chair, and wide-screen, Harris believed he was headed away from being president of anything.

After sitting in the car for twenty minutes, the setting sun broke through the dark, receding clouds. Harris had enough sitting in Mrs. Filbert's smelly car and thinking about his life. He pushed open the door and heard another vehicle approach on the main road. It stopped near Mrs. Filbert's car.

"Hi ho," Danny yelled, jumping out of his boss' wrecker.

Harris wished the boss man Sam had come instead. Danny liked to call himself a "free spirit," which really meant he was reckless in everything he did.

Harris got out of the car, pushing his wide black shoes into the muddy ground. He wondered if Mrs. Filbert would miss her car if it sank in the mud and disappeared.

"Hi, ho, Harris. You're still as ugly as ever."

"Stop with the 'hi ho' crap. I'm not one of the seven dwarfs. You come to tow Mrs. Filbert's car away?"

"Yeah. Jeff called to tell me about it. Where you want it towed?" Danny grinned like the mischievous Cheshire Cat.

Harris thought that if he had it towed to Mrs. Filbert's house, he'd have a junk sitting there drawing complaints. If he got it towed to Sam's Garage, Sam wouldn't work on it. He knew Mrs. Filbert would send the bill to the treasurer who Sam knew was Harris and that the association had no money. Harris figured he had a good chance of being stuck with the broken car where it was and drawing lawsuit threats from trailer owners who would not vote him out of office.

As he scratched his fingers through his wiry head of dark hair, sending flakes of dandruff across his cheekbones, Harris heard someone walking down Majestic Avenue toward him. That person had a happy skip in their step.

"Hey, Harris," Jeff said. "We did it. Me and Mrs. Filbert, or Bertha as I'll call her."

"Did what?" Harris hoped it was not murder. He didn't want to find another vice president.

"She was hot for me when we got to her place. Heavy rain like that makes her horny. Man, she was all over me. Hey, hey. Damn good thing I'm blind. Feisty old women are the best. Very limber."

"Hey, Jeff. This Danny. You wanna drive my boss' wrecker around? I wanna see a blind man drive."

"Hell, yeah, you dumb ass."

"Hey! We gotta get Mrs. Filbert's car outta here," Harris said.

"We'll be back," Danny said as he led Jeff toward the truck.

In quick order, Jeff jumped in the driver's seat with Danny beside him. Harris watched them fight over the steering wheel as a loud grinding of gears echoed across the trailer park entrance. Eventually, the tow truck swerved into the roadway and disappeared around a bend in the road.

The squealing sound of the wrecker's tires receded away from Harris as he turned around to the sound of someone else coming down Majestic Avenue. He hoped it was the extraterrestrial to take him off the planet.

"Stand back, you damn ugly fool. I'm limbered up and I'm goin' get my damn car outta here," said Mrs. Filbert.

The old woman wore a thin frock that left her sagging boobs flopping around like boxing gloves. At the car door, she kicked off mud from her bulky black shoes and threw in her cane and crutch before plopping behind the steering wheel.

"Mrs. Filbert, I don't think that car's drivable."

"Shut up, damn you. Did I ask for your damn opinion? And clean up all this damn mud, damn it. Or, I'll sue!"

A grating noise shuddered and spat the car's engine into a questionable life. A loud clunk of shifting gears and the smell of vaporized metal shavings hung in the moist air as Harris jumped back. He watched Mrs. Filbert crush the gas pedal, spin mud from the bald tires, and send the grinding sound of metal on bricks high into the humid twilight air.

The battered car tore from its perch against the brick pillar and burst onto Majestic Avenue in a chaos of noise, smoke, and mud. Harris watched the gray mound of Mrs. Filbert's head as she peered over the top of the steering wheel and drove into Trailer Paradise. Harris thought she looked like a white-haired vampire bat returning to its cave.

With the sound of her car's pain fading into the damp air, Harris discovered himself standing alone at the entrance to Majestic Avenue. Dark clouds loomed in the distance, mud was everywhere, and a scattering of broken bricks lay on the ground. The sudden silence of his surroundings made him feel tired as the sun began to set.

He gazed at the broken ladder and scattered bricks and had no motivation to clean things up. *I'll come back tomorrow morning,* he told himself, wishing he cared less about being president. *Maybe I can get Jeff to help if I promise not to make him*

VP next year, Harris considered. Yeah, that's it. I'll make him president and I'll be VP.

Harris walked home as the rain started again, this time more gently. He thought about visiting Mrs. Filbert, but he was ugly, not blind. He let the rain push across his face and tumble down his coat that he wished was some kind of tweed.

A few feet in front of his trailer, Harris met the groundhog Potter. The overweight animal stared at the three metal steps leading up to the wet veneer door of his singlewide.

"What do you want?" Harris wondered if anyone would notice a groundhog as president of the association.

Potter glanced over its shoulder at Harris, like a child to a parent, and waddled closer to the metal stairs. Harris frowned as the splatter of rain pinged off metal trailer roofs throughout Trailer Paradise.

"You're wet and you smell. I'm not bringing you in my new house. Go find your hole."

Potter stood motionless, staring up at the three metal stairs.

They were both getting wetter. Harris let out a heavy sigh. "Knowing you, your hole is probably flooded. You need to dig a home on higher ground."

With the rain coming down heavier, Harris walked over and picked Potter up in one swoop.

Inside his trailer, Harris grabbed a towel and dried the animal's fur as best he could. Then he stripped off his clothes, leaving them on the kitchen floor, and put on his long cotton bathrobe. Picking up Potter, Harris plopped down in his red leather chair covered in plastic with the groundhog in his lap.

Harris felt Potter's bristly fur and warm body. He felt comfort from the animal's warmth.

"You can stay here tonight, but tomorrow you need to dig a better hole. Maybe I'll help you," Harris said, wishing Potter understood.

The groundhog nestled further onto Harris' lap. From a cooler next to his chair, Harris pulled out the first of a six-pack of beer. Half of the can he shared with Potter, who opened his mouth when Harris started to pour. Soon Potter was snoring in Harris' lap.

He flipped on the big screen TV that came with special functions for strong colors. Harris found the black and white movie *Night of the Living Dead* as he got into his second beer. Watching the opening credits, he started thinking about his permanent ugliness and lack of a family.

"Maybe I could have adopted my father. No one ever said an orphan couldn't adopt someone instead of being adopted himself," Harris said to Potter.

The groundhog raised its head and Harris gave the animal a hug. The smelly creature did this rare, special thing of almost hugging back. Then, it went back to snoring.

While staring at the dead gray people moping around on his color TV, Harris said to himself, "I'll make Potter the Treasurer since there's no money. No one will notice."

He watched the stiff-walking ghouls in the movie beat on the house near the graveyard. Harris imagined trailer court residents beating on his door, threatening to sue if their pointless complaints were not met.

By the third beer, Harris fell asleep in his red leather lounge chair on Majestic Avenue on the outskirts of Trailer Paradise with Potter warm and snoring in his lap.

Dusty Light Bulbs

I read an article about a woman obsessed with cleaning light bulbs. She aggravated her family, who tolerated this only obsession. She had three daughters and became a grandmother and great-grandmother that everyone loved. When she died, her daughters continued the tradition of cleaning their light bulbs. At least for a little while.

While she was married, Betsy kept all the light bulbs in their one-bedroom apartment polished. A day would not go by without the flick of a dust rag on the lamp bulbs or the ceiling lights where she needed the foot stool. There was hardly any dust in the apartment—she kept the place too clean. It was the thought of any tiny particle filtering the light and clouding her life.

Now, two years later after her wedding, dust covered the light bulbs as she sat at the kitchen table making decisions alone.

That morning, a week after she last cleaned the apartment, Betsy imagined dust piling on the light bulbs and dimming the artificial glare falling on her. She imagined being bathed in shadows everywhere. She wished there were more shadows to hide what she had on the table.

A cardboard storage box beside her held stuff she no longer wanted. At the bottom of the box was a thick book about trains her husband read like some people read the bible. On top of that were pictures from her wedding day. On top of the pictures and book, she placed her husband's obituary from the local newspaper.

The obit described his birth date, death date, parents living as expats in rural Asia, she being his surviving wife, and how Harold had worked as a freight train apprentice. Betsy still hadn't found his parents to tell them, if they cared. The obit did not mention a funeral. Betsy had no one to invite.

She sat there thinking about things until noon, when she left the apartment and walked outside into the bright sun. Betsy took a light coat because it would be chilly later in the evening.

Before leaving, she made sure the apartment lights were off. She did not want anyone noticing the lights did not shine as bright as they should. Walking down the broken sidewalk, Betsy thought about how people who lived in shadows had secrets and lacked commitment.

It took her five hours to walk the eleven miles. Not owning a car, she could have taken a city cab or bus or some other hired transportation, but she did not. She was not sure the quick ride in any of them would have given her enough time to properly judge her life or the decisions she had made. It felt better to walk and walk and walk. It helped build her courage as she reached her destination.

Even walking, Betsy arrived before she wanted. She approached the cemetery surrounded by four short walls of large, misshapen stones. Inside the walls was a weed covered ground with maybe a hundred headstones of granite and marble sprouting up. Weeds and moss assumed authority over most of the headstones, making them seem like another type of weed.

Outside the stone perimeter, a sparse forest of underbrush and old-growth trees encroached in three directions. Except in the front, where the rusted iron gate assembly faced the narrow city road. The entrance was the only evidence that an old cemetery was there.

Betsy didn't know any of the people buried there. Except for one. She moved around to the back wall, where she could get a better view of her husband's new granite headstone. It stood out among older ones like a shiny light bulb. One day it would be as moss covered and stained as the others and be nothing worth remembering.

She sensed old ghosts telling her to go away. At the back wall, Betsy found an old, four-door sedan among the bushes and trees. The car had deflated tires melted into the forest floor with tree limbs drooping over the rusted, yellow body. The car was built when cars were long and wide, elegant, and stylish.

Since it would get dark soon, Betsy tightened her light coat around her small body, threw loose stones and twigs inside the abandoned car to chase out any small animals, and slipped through the broken back window. She buried herself in dead leaves and plant debris as the cool night air moved in.

With the descending darkness, she hummed old folk songs and consumed her chocolate bars and bottled water she brought with her. She didn't emerge until the morning sun was high enough to reheat the stagnant air.

Betsy again looked just over the edge of the stone wall at her husband's granite headstone and the freshly turned mound of clay soil. She still could not convince herself to enter the cemetery and tread on ground so close to his headstone. She felt safer in the shadow of the old trees and near the old car.

She looked up into the jagged limbs hanging over her head as squirrels and birds looked down. In the distance, Betsy listened to a train horn toot.

Before long, Betsy watched an elderly woman with stale flowers come to the cemetery. She caught sight of Betsy peering just over the wall's edge. Fifteen minutes later, the local police found Betsy, who had returned to the inside of the abandoned car.

Sitting in the back seat and looking through the cracked front window, she watched two policemen approach. Closing her eyes and taking a deep breath, Betsy remembered when her life started to bring her to this moment.

At sixteen, her dad died when he drove his pickup across train tracks in front of a fast-moving freight train. The train passed through the pickup he was riding in as if it wasn't there. Betsy's dad gave her so little attention that she cried terribly, knowing he would never get the chance to make up for his lack of affection toward her. Betsy's mother never said where he was going or if anyone else was riding with him.

A sudden loss of income brought Mother and Betsy to live on grandfather's crop farm where Mother grew up. Of the things Betsy remembered most was the sweet smell of summer thunderstorms. She would run into the nearby clover fields to stand among the small purplish flowers as jagged daggers of light streaked across the cloudy sky.

Betsy raised her arms and spread her legs to make an X. She stretched out as far as she could, letting the tiny scars on the back of her legs from her grandfather's willow switch disappear—almost.

She had no fear of the violent storms. They gave her courage. As the hanging clouds unleashed their rain and drenched the teenage Betsy, she imagined escaping the pain of her existence. She wanted the rain and wind to pick her up and carry her above the grim loneliness of the decaying farm. When the storm ended, she returned to the farmhouse, disappointed there was no other place to go.

"We've got to live here 'cause your father left us no money," Mother told Betsy after a particularly vicious storm flattened some of the crops. Her grandfather yelled about how much he hated Betsy and his daughter living there, costing him money.

"Why don't you get a job? I know why. It's because you think by staying here you'll inherit this place when they're gone," Betsy yelled at her mother.

"I deserve this place after what I tolerated growing up here," she yelled back.

"You're too scared to leave. You're too scared to keep that old man from hitting me. If there's one thing I'm going to do, it's to get off this crummy farm and not be scared, not even of your father," Betsy continued to yell.

She said this loud enough for Grandfather to hear in the next room. He would know she was not taking any more abuse from him, and he did not dare confront her or say anything since. As a high school junior, Betsy decided she was woman enough to defy the people who kept her trapped as a girl. Soon after, she dated Harold, a high school senior.

Harold wanted to be a train engineer when he graduated. Betsy wondered if she could like trains and a day after she turned eighteen, she quit school to marry Harold to find out.

"I have a marriage to work on so don't depend on me helping you, Mother," Betsy said as she was leaving.

She left her mother on a farm with more weeds than crops, a grandmother who needed help eating breakfast, and a grandfather who stayed in the barn drinking his vodka.

Betsy remembered all this as the two police officers now stood outside her car talking into small black boxes on their shoulders. She closed her eyes, trying to wish them away as she remembered her marriage.

In the one-bedroom apartment where she lived with her husband, Betsy kept the light bulbs clean. Brightness meant no secrets and that was the key to a healthy marriage, she believed. This helped her adjust to being a woman and a wife.

The first year, Harold got a job around a train yard helping to lash up locomotives for high priority, hot shot freight trains. It gave him driving experience and Betsy was proud of how quickly he moved up to being an apprentice hostler.

She filled her days working in a small women's clothing store within walking distance from the apartment. The store owner had hoped to expand, yet Betsy never saw enough customers to keep the current store running.

In the second year, Harold rode low priority dog trains around the city as a first step to being a train engineer. Except, he gathered a lot of time waiting in a hole or side track for hot shot trains to pass.

"It won't be long before I'm driving my own hot shot freight train and passing those dog trains," Harold told Betsy many times at supper.

After the clothing store closed, Betsy worked as a waitress in a nearby diner. She came home smelling of the foul words from anxious eaters while Harold worked extra hours to get ahead.

She often sat waiting in the empty apartment until the early morning hours. When Harold came home, he smelled like soot and grime from a diesel locomotive. Yet, she felt a pain move through her head. Mentally harsh, like there was another smell that shouldn't be there.

Each morning, Betsy experienced Harold's departure without a time for his return. When home, he never mentioned the brightness she created in the apartment with the clean light bulbs. Instead, he cut off the bright lights, leaving only shadows. He managed in the dim twilight better than she.

One evening as he gulped down his supper, she asked Harold, "What's it like to ride a freight train?"

"It's big, noisy, and smelly. You get dirty as soon as you step inside. Those hot shot trains got clean insides. My broken padded seat makes my butt sore and we break down all the time. Those hot shot trains got cushioned seats and get priority for fixin' that ours don't. I'm moving on from this job real soon. I'm moving up to them hot shot trains where I'll get respect. I'm going places."

"What's going to happen when you move up?"

Harold kept eating.

"Maybe when you move up, you can be home more," Betsy said.

"Don't push me right now. I'm goin' to get my priorities straight first. Once I get on a hot shot train, I'm goin' to be away more. I don't want you whining when that happens 'cause it'll get us out of this apartment faster, like you want."

She didn't want that. She liked their small apartment. Betsy watched him finish eating his steak and potato supper by running his bread around the plate and soaking up what remained. His plate looked clean. As he showered, she put the plate away without washing it like she usually did. They went to bed, yet she kept awake until hearing his heavy breathing.

Harold mumbled in his sleep, but Betsy could understand enough. A few days before his death, he would whisper how he had no dreams, only goals and desires to be a hero to himself. His words were like a chant, motivating him to continue with his life. In the morning, Betsy held her tears until he was gone to work.

One of the police officers interrupted Betsy's memories by tapping on the car's broken door to get her attention. She ignored him and buried herself further into the dead leaves and debris while thinking about when Harold did not come home.

That night, the apartment felt to Betsy like a closed box. Searching for a warm feeling of space, she pulled up the apartment's only window and hung her head out. The acrid wind from the soiled city caressed her face. In the distance, she heard the low rumble of a freight train making its passage through the tall buildings.

The sound came low at first, pushing back the stinking air, before growing into a defiant noise echoing off the decaying buildings around her. The rumbling train receded quickly from its climax, letting out a long blast of a horn like saying goodbye to the city's clutches. Because Harold feared technology, they only had a landline phone that rang, pulling Betsy away from the window.

She stood in the kitchen grasping the handheld receiver as a man's hoarse voice explained about Harold's death. Betsy looked down at her white dress with a slight color of blue on the embroidered hem and tight sleeves. She would not wear that dress again.

The next day, Betsy walked around the apartment in one of Harold's shirts that swallowed her body from neck to feet. She drank hot black coffee and ate stale sugar cookies while letting the light bulbs gather dust. What was the last thing Harold thought before dying, she wondered? What was the last thing he smelled and what did he hear as his life ceased to exist?

A week after she placed the phone receiver onto its cradle, silencing the official voice on the other end, the dusty apartment lights watched Betsy place Harold's things in the cardboard box. What she didn't place in the box was a print-out of his emails and his diary, which she stacked on the table next to the storage box.

The emails were in one stack and organized by date to create a timeline of where along the train tracks Harold met the woman. Except now there was little to read.

Betsy had used a permanent marker to black out the woman's name wherever she saw it. Then she blacked out comments the other woman made to Harold. Finally, Betsy blacked out what Harold wrote to that woman. She had a lot of paper with long, thick, black stripes.

Next to the emails, Betsy did not use the marker on Harold's diary. Instead, she left exposed the entries where he explained how his dog train would sit in a hole for hours off a spur from the main line. That was where he met the other woman coming across the tracks from an apartment building so old it had been upgraded twice without success.

In his diary, he made excuses and complained how management would not get him on a hot shot train for years. He couldn't think that far ahead, Harold wrote. I want things now.

With troubled handwriting, his last diary entry was barely readable. Yet, knowing her husband, Betsy could read how he planned to run away with this woman. He would work for another train company with a better chance of riding a hot shot train.

That night they were to leave, he wrote how he watched his woman step onto a rain soaked steel track trying to reach his dog train. She stumbled into the path of a hot shot, fast moving freight train.

It was not a direct hit and she died on the way to the hospital. Betsy read this in a newspaper article describing the accident. The article said the woman died alone, like Betsy was feeling while putting Harold's possessions in the cardboard box that morning. On top of his obituary, she put the letter from the railroad company.

It explained how, after Harold's dog train pulled into the train yard, he got out and walked in front of an Amtrak locomotive heading south.

The letter did not say how his body made little noise against the aerodynamic locomotive. The funeral director told her that. He was trying to be sympathetic and explain how Harold died instantly, without pain. She wished he had died knowing he was dying.

The passenger train was several hours late to its next destination. They had to clean Harold's remains off the front of the locomotive's cowling before moving to the next station. Betsy wondered why didn't the Amtrak take Harold's remains along.

That morning she left the apartment, Betsy left the box, printed-out emails, and Harold's diary to suffer under the dusty lights.

She was startled back into her present situation when other police officers tried opening the car doors, which had not been opened for a long time. They decided not to risk coming in like she did through the rusted metal and broken glass. She heard more sirens heading her way.

Betsy ignored all of this and remembered how much she wanted a funeral for her husband. She called her mother for advice. Still living on the old farm with old parents, her mother said, "Now that your man is dead, come back to the farm. I need help dealing with all this old."
"I got to have a funeral for my husband."

"I didn't have one for your father. You know why? I'll tell you anyway. Yeah, he died when a train hit his truck. 'Cept, he was drunk and loving on a local whore and didn't see the train coming." Mother chuckled, the wicked kind.

Betsy worked on forgetting about her mother as more people approached her abandoned car. A man, overly dressed as a firefighter with no fire around to put out, began prying open a rear door. Other police and firefighters came to watch. Betsy yelled at them to leave her alone.

Popping her head out of the dead leaves and debris, she explained to them, "I have a right to be here. That's my husband's headstone in the cemetery."

"Why don't you come out of the car? We'll get you some help," said a policewoman through the back window.

"I don't need any help. I've already taken care of everything. You see, my mother had no funeral for my dad and there's no gravesite for me to visit. I wanted a gravesite for my husband. A place where I could visit and tell him what he's missing by being dead."

Betsy had to shout over the firefighter's prying tool. "The cemetery people wouldn't let me put up a headstone unless I had a coffin to bury. There wasn't enough of my husband's body to put in a coffin."

The policewoman signaled for the firefighter to stop so everyone could listen. Betsy sat up straight, leaning against the broken springs of the back seat, and shouted out the window.

"At the morgue, no one wanted that woman's body, so I claimed it. I put her in a cheap coffin and buried her in the cemetery so I could have a headstone with my husband's name on it." Betsy chuckled, much like her mother.

"I came here to visit my husband's headstone. But the ghost of that woman buried there stopped me. I can feel her resentment over what I did. There's got to be something funny about all of this."

Office Primitive

I worked way too many decades in the Pentagon. This is so much like what really goes on in the puzzle palace.

"I hate Atlanta. I'm moving to Miami with Harry," Charlie's wife Henrietta said as she finished putting suitcases and boxes into the back of Harry's SUV.

"If you move away, I won't see the kids." Charlie was not liking this divorce thing or his wife's new boyfriend Harry, who was the reason for the divorce.

"The kids will live with me and Harry. They'll visit you on the schedule we came up with. It's settled."

Charlie stood on the front porch waving goodbye to his daughters, fourteen-year-old Prisha and twelve-year-old Samantha. No one waved back. They continued leaving with their new father, Harry.

Charlie wondered if the melancholy thing he had going on might have had something to do with his daughters' changing allegiance toward a more cheerful, manly person. Changing allegiances bothered Charlie, particularly when he ended up without one. It made him melancholy.

The next day, after "The Leaving" as Charlie called it, he went to his melancholy job. He found no solace working for the Sorbet Bloozteria Company. Headed by CEO Georgiana Sorbet, she wanted women to be free of childbirth, which meant impregnating men. Or something else. It was the "something else" that worried Charlie. Well, impregnating men bothered him, too.

No one knew what motivated CEO Sorbet to stop women from birthing babies. She was not against babies, just the birthing part. It was rumored she had a daughter and maybe the experience traumatized CEO Sorbet. Charlie wondered what trauma the daughter felt for having Georgiana Sorbet as a mother.

Across the street was Granite Company, headed by Marge Willywrighter. She challenged her employees to "Make a Better Quality of Life." Charlie thought he would enjoy tracking budget numbers under Marge. Except he was working for Georgiana.

Each day in his cubicle, Charlie worked at keeping budgets from adopting a minus sign. Yet, he had trouble concentrating after overhearing co-worker Janet from the other side of their shared cubicle wall. For a woman-owned office, the organization had a lot of male bosses and she had a talent to get these men to do things for her. Maybe Georgiana planned to impregnate these male bosses, which Charlie thought would be a good idea.

One day while sitting in his cubicle and trying not to listen to Janet coo on some boss, Charlie emailed his spreadsheets to his three supervisors. He wanted them to know about minus signs lurking in the numbers. Except, management gave the data to Janet to summarize.

Her summaries added theoretical profits from a secret project called Quicksilver only she knew about. Management liked Janet's summaries with theories and secrets and no threat of minus signs. Charlie feared Janet would become his boss one day. It made him melancholy.

The next morning, big boss Jenkins emailed Janet, Charlie, and three others. He explained in the email, "Our profit maker Quicksilver needs cash so it can continue as a profit maker. I selected all of you for team Mercury to identify company projects to fund Quicksilver. Let's have a start-up meeting on this in an hour."

The meeting was held at ten o'clock in the conference room where the Mercury team faced each other for the first time. Sally was always early for meetings and came in first. Even on her worse days, Charlie thought she looked better than Janet, who came in next looking like she would throw something at Sally for being first. Stu followed the women, keeping lustful glances at their bodies until Patterson, of pasty-look fame, used his round wideness to block Stu's view. Charlie came in last, thinking he was entering a carnival sideshow.

The polished, long conference room table dominated the room. It was surrounded with enough chairs to host three times as many people and the multiple seating choices ran confusion through the team who stood around avoiding eye contact. Except for Patterson, who slumped in the nearest chair like a dollop of goop plopping down.

Jenkins strode into the room like he was Napoleon ready to conquer France. He followed Patterson's lead and landed in an end chair nearby. The others made their seating decisions as Patterson said, "I looked it up and quicksilver is another name for the chemical element mercury."

This broke protocol by not letting Jenkins speak first, and it prompted a sneer from Janet.

"Don't confuse things with chemical names," Janet said. She wiggled her painted fingernail at Patterson. He started giggling when her fake nail broke loose and flopped around.

"Let's get to work," demanded Jenkins. "As the Mercury team, we need to make Quicksilver successful." He sounded like they were heroes in a comic book and about to save the Earth.

"What does Quicksilver do?" Patterson inhaled through his nose with a loud sucking sound and he seemed to enjoy swallowing the snot he sucked in.

"Quicksilver is close-hold and a secret," said Janet. She twisted in her chair to face Jenkins more and Patterson less.

"Quicksilver sounds like a stink to me," said Stu, licking his lips and eyeing Sally. She gave Stu a look that she would kick the crap out of him if he didn't stop leering at her.

Jenkins concentrated on his reflection in the polished conference room table as Janet leaned close. She planned to whisper something to him just as his neck bulged. He burped. A loud, stinky kind that struck Janet full in the face. They all watched her jump out of the chair and run out of the room, holding her mouth to keep from vomiting. Without Janet, Jenkins seemed to lose his confidence to lead, and he adjourned the meeting.

Charlie wished all his meetings were this efficient and short.

That week, he worked a step-by-step process to locate company projects to fund Quicksilver. There were a lot of projects with generic titles, as if camouflaging what they did. And way too many losing money. Charlie wondered if the projects could all be the same, just under different generic names.

He examined three databases and used algorithms he didn't really understand to search for accounts not already in accounting trouble. In his search through the databases, Charlie discovered that Sorbet Bloozteria, as an engineering consultant firm, employed few engineering consultants. Also, most of the income came from an unknown outside source that funded Quicksilver. His biggest concern were the U.S. military intelligence contracts he found.

They were obvious with mostly blank pages labeled U.S. Military Intelligence Contract. Charlie googled the contract numbers and found they originated from a military deception office in southern Maryland.

Charlie didn't want to be employed by a secret military project. He couldn't tolerate working for a company that was a phantom company and did not really exist. He needed to talk to someone about what he found. Charlie called Sally that night, knowing she lived alone.

"Keep it to yourself for now until you know more. There's other things going on in the company and maybe it all ties in together," she advised. "On another subject, how's your divorce going?"

"It'll soon be final. Are you still dating that guy in IT?"

"No. Turns out he was married and wanted me as his playmate. When I found out, I explained to his wife that I'm not playmate material. She relayed the message to him with the divorce papers. Anyway, I got to go. My girlfriends and I are having dinner and drinks tonight."

Seeking more relief from what he found out, Charlie spent the weekend video chatting with his daughters. They told him how much fun they had on a deep-sea fishing trip with Harry. Charlie could not get past the thought of barbed hooks in his daughters' hands as they bounced on ocean waves. Harry was taking them on unsafe journeys Charlie wished he had taken them on.

On Monday afternoon, Janet popped her head into Charlie's cubicle, startling him. He jumped.

"I just got back from a meeting with Jenkins. How are you doing on Mercury?" Janet stood with her hands on hips like Superwoman.

Charlie wished he did not live in a cubicle universe where doors did not exist. He told Janet, "Don't worry. I'm ready to send out a macro instruction to temporarily replace accounts randomly with pre-positioned numbers. Reality has no chance here."

Janet stomped away with her bottom lip stuck out.

"To achieve an outcome, control will be relinquished and confusion installed," Charlie said to her receding backside.

An hour before quitting time, Jenkins appeared at Charlie's doorless cubicle. Janet stood close behind, peering over Jenkin's shoulder.

"The chief wants to see charts on Mercury by Thursday AM," Jenkins said. "Read-aheads are due 24 hours prior, so on Wednesday AM. The VP is doing the briefing and he needs to look at them a day before for his prep. I, as Mercury team leader, and Janet as executive secretary of the team, need them the day before. What can we do to help?"

Charlie stopped typing and faced his helpers. "If the charts are due Thursday, read-aheads are due on Wednesday, the vice president wants them a day early, and you two want them the day before that, that makes it Monday. Today is Monday and it's almost quitting time. Did you know that?"

"Yes, what can we do to help?" Janet scrunched her face into an impression of anger, hate, and general disgust toward Charlie for pointing this out.

"Let's call in Sally, Patterson, and Stu to help since they're on the team, too," said Charlie.

Jenkins cleared his throat and said, "I think we can readjust the schedule and deadlines."

As the two walked away, Charlie knew they would blame him for the schedule delays. He considered telling them he already had the charts done, but that wouldn't have been any fun. Right at quitting time, he had Stu deliver eleven printed charts to Jenkins. Sally met Charlie and Patterson in the lunchroom to explain Stu's delivery.

"As Stu was about to walk into Jenkins' office with the charts, Janet confronted him and tried to take the charts. Stu refused. Jenkins came out to find out what was going on and Janet, trying to stay between the two men, stepped back and her heel went into Jenkin's shoe. This made Jenkins to pull his foot away causing Janet to stumble forward into Stu. He caught her squarely in the boobies."

"Stu's not on our team anymore," Sally concluded.

Patterson couldn't stop giggling at the word "boobies."

That Friday, neither Jenkins nor Janet told Charlie what happened at the meeting where his charts were used. So, he got the agenda and saw that his charts were not on the itinerary, but Janet's were. Later, he got a copy of the charts and they were his with her name on them.

On Monday morning, Sally came into Charlie's cubicle and spread a draft organizational chart across his cubicle shelf. Fortunately, he had nothing there. He liked that Sally was sharing her discovery with him. They were sharing a lot of discoveries lately.

"Where do we fit in with the new organization?" She didn't seem to notice that Charlie's cubicle was barely big enough for him.

"Let's see. This one is a general manager, and this other one is a general manager. General manager, general manager, general manager," Charlie said. He looked for his and Sally's position in the long, fold out hierarchy and wondered if their positions were in one of the creases.

"What about these over here?" Sally pointed to the positions directly above Charlie's big hand.

"Directors, directors, directors." Charlie hammered his index finger into each tiny box like poking a needle into a voodoo doll. "Many directors because of so many managers. Looks like one analyst to an average of four managers and three directors." Charlie held his palm up to Sally's face in a gesture of stop talking. A deep male voice seeped through the large cloth wall he shared with Janet.

"Burn daylight, but it's not going to be a dog and pony show. Dig down in the dirt and show them what we're standing on," said the male voice Charlie did not recognize.

He cupped his ear against the coarse cloth wall so he could hear better and did not notice Sally walking away with her chart. He had a hard time making out both conversations, anyway.

"You can't let this reorganization get out. Let me talk to it," said Janet. He lost the rest when she lowered her voice.

Frustrated that he could not hear, Charlie went online and searched for listening devices so he could maybe find out what Quicksilver was about. He found a device cheap enough and could be delivered by Friday. That way I can install it after everyone leaves, he thought. He bought The Ear.

The Ear is Super Bionic! It listens through any surface, and the earplugs fit discreetly into normal or deformed ears. Just place the amplifier next to the listening surface and hear what you should not be hearing!

Charlie liked that he could get a bionic ear. He installed it that Friday night after work and on Monday morning he shoved the small round plugs into his ears. Flipping on The Ear gave an immediate high-pitched squeal so that for an hour he could not hear people talking to him who stood a foot away.

Did Janet have an anti-bionic ear device hidden in her cubicle? When she went to lunch, Charlie snuck into her cubicle and looked around, finding nothing. Except, he did spy an invoice for body fluids, specifically urine and blood samples, from a local funeral home.

The invoice looked so ridiculous that Charlie figured it had to be a fake. Besides, if he told anyone, Janet would know he was spying on her. Back at his cubicle, he pulled out the instructions from the trash can and read how he should not put The Ear within ten feet of other electronic equipment. Looking around, electronic equipment surrounded him.

He put the device in the supply closet that no one ever looked in. Everyone used computers and had no need for office supplies.

The next day, Jenkins emailed everyone on the Mercury team to a one o'clock meeting. They milled around in the same conference room where the previous attendees had left paper cups of cold coffee and small wrappers labeled with calories in the 200s. Charlie thought of overweight insomniacs.

Jenkins said, "An issue has come up and we need a quick cash infusion for Quicksilver."

"We're ready to run that Mercury drill," Janet called out like a hurrah.

"Do that Mercury thing, now." Jenkins said with a click of his tongue. He disappeared from his leather chair and out the door.

"You heard him. Execute Quicksilver. I mean Mercury," Janet told the three as she chased after Jenkins.

"I'm confused. Either of you know how to do that?" Patterson asked as he leaned a little to the side as if getting ready to fart.

Charlie explained about the unknown outside source funding Quicksilver.

"That's easy, then," said Patterson. "Get the outside source to donate more money."

"I don't know who that source is," Charlie said. "Instead, I'm proposing taking eleven and one eighth percent from every account that has a plus sign. That way people will think there was some thought put behind the reductions. I'll put the money into a temporary account labeled Mercury until I find out what Quicksilver is about."

"Sounds safer that way," said Sally.

She and Charlie left the room because Patterson had farted.

Saturday, Charlie's daughters emailed him to say they were staying for four weeks. He was overcome with worry, wondering if he could control his melancholy with his daughters visiting and while doing the Mercury drill.

He met his daughters the next day at the airport. They came through the terminal with Prisha in the lead and Samantha following.

"Dad, I'm on my period and I don't feel like eating anything," Prisha announced. "I'm so bloated I can't stand it. Look at my fat legs and my butt."

Charlie saw no need to view his daughter that way. He stared at Samantha for help.

"Hi, Dad. Got any munchies in the car?"

Charlie wanted to give skinny Prisha a bag of chips and chunky Samantha a low-calorie pretzel. He worried that understanding daughters was going to be harder than he thought. Whether he was melancholy or not.

Walking out of the terminal, Charlie wanted a topic for them to talk about on the ride home. "I'm working on a special project at work."

"We don't care about your boring job, Dad," Prisha said.

"That's Dad you're talking to," Samantha sounded as if her dad was too old to have hearing. "Dad's not like that other guy Mom is living with."

Charlie was happier carrying heavy travel bags to the car. He was still physically stronger than they, even if it meant carrying cosmetics, hair dryers, and extra bras that made his daughters seem stronger than him.

"I don't understand men," said Prisha, pulling out her smartphone on the drive home.

"They have no understanding of anything. Dad, you got the better end of the divorce," Samantha said, pulling out her smartphone.

Charlie would have kissed the inventor of the smartphone. They gave his daughters something to do besides talking about the current situation none of them wanted to talk about.

On Monday morning, the vice president of human resources did not announce the reorganization. He merely emailed one-pagers showing an organization chart with names. Half the people did not realize their names were not there. They tried to access their computer accounts and a call to the help desk explained everything, like a data point.

Charlie, Sally, and Patterson read the chart carefully before barging into Jenkins's office.

"Why aren't we on the new org chart?" Sally slapped her hand on Jenkins' desk.

"Look at this as an opportunity." He stared at his monitor, which was turned off.

"You're working for Janet," Patterson said. "I saw her name above yours."

Jenkins hesitated before saying, "Janet did not take my promotion. Yes, she'll be telling me what to do, but I'm a leader. I can find other opportunities just like each of you should."

The next morning, several former employees of Sorbet Bloozteria filled out applications before being ushered into the introduction room of Granite Company. Ms. Willywrighter greeted them by welcoming their talents. Charlie never met Ms.

Sorbet. He knew her only by the faded, stained picture in the men's bathroom.

"I'm in," Sally told Charlie afterwards. "I've got enough computer skills to work in their IT department."

"They need a numbers person and they're sending me to train on their budget software," Charlie said.

Patterson walked over to them. "They're sending me to supervisory training."

After the meeting, Charlie met Ms. Willywrighter and immediately forgot his melancholy thing. The budget software would let Charlie work at home. Marge told him to take time with his daughters after he explained his situation.

Over the next month, Charlie still did not understand periods and emotions, but he was glad his daughters enjoyed staying with him. At the end of the month, his ex gave up custody. She found happiness living with a guy who supervised construction workers. Also, she did not have to bother with teenage children. Henrietta lived in a house with bars on the windows, huge flying cockroaches circling, alligators lurking in the swamps, and hot sticky heat—it all suited her.

At this same time, the news media erupted with stories about the financial collapse of Sorbet Bloozteria. This was not unexpected. What made the news was Janet's social media posts blaming her male bosses for sexual harassment. Mostly it was true. However, the male bosses had recorded Janet's harassment on them, which made her guilty in 3-D.

A few days later at lunch, Sally shared with Charlie and Patterson what she found out after talking to Jenkins.

"He's telling everyone everything to keep from going to jail. He told me that investigators found funeral home invoices in Janet's office. She had been taking money from Quicksilver to buy body fluids. Her plan was to use electricity and slather urine and blood from cadavers over human eggs to grow an embryo. I think Janet saw too many Frankenstein movies," said Sally.

"Did the body fluids have anything to do with freeing women from childbirth?" Patterson asked, chomping down on his corned beef sandwich. They were all enjoying the cafeteria food cooked by a real chef.

"She might have thought so," said Sally, enjoying her spicy Asian salad.

"I ask because I think her project was a way to please her mother," said Patterson, taking another chomp on his fatty sandwich.

Charlie and Sally looked at each other before Sally asked, "Whose mother?"

"In management training, I heard gossip that Janet was doing all of this to please her mother Georgiana."

Charlie couldn't finish his grilled cheese sandwich, even though it had real cheese. Before he was laid off, he got The Ear to work from his cubicle and he realized now that he was spying on Sorbet's daughter.

He remembered Janet on the phone telling someone that, if her project worked, she wanted to be changed back to a male she was born as. She apparently needed approval before having a sex reassignment procedure. Charlie realized Janet was talking to her mother, Georgiana Sorbet.

While Sally and Patterson traded gossip, Charlie sat there wondering why Georgiana would change her son into a daughter. Likely when Janet was very young. And why did Georgiana have contracts with military intelligence? Was Quicksilver a means for the military to invest in the Sorbet Bloozteria company?

That afternoon, Charlie accessed the local library's online archives using special access he discovered while working for

Sorbet Bloozteria. He found newspaper articles and police records revealing that Georgiana became pregnant after being raped. Charlie believed Georgiana didn't want to free women from childbirth. She wanted men to go through childbirth if they raped a woman. But why change Janet from a boy to a girl?

He could only assume Georgiana did not want her son to grow up and rape a woman. Charlie figured her son probably looked like the rapist and she feared he would turn out like his father. Janet wanted to be changed back, but only if her mother accepted her as a son.

That evening, Charlie invited Sally to an Italian restaurant so she could help him figure the rest out.

"I found out more from Jenkins," said Sally, slurping a noodle.

"Let's start with Quicksilver," said Charlie. He took a napkin, reached across the table, and wiped sauce from Sally's chin. She smiled.

"It all started when Sorbet Bloozteria needed cash and the military needed a phantom company to run a deception through. Quicksilver was the account the military used to fund the company," said Sally.

"So, all those generic projects I found were fake," said Charlie.

"Not all of them. Some were Georgiana Sorbet's projects to free women of childbirth. Janet found out about Quicksilver and she took some of the money for her project. She wanted to satisfy her mother with her own accomplishments. Janet figured the military would replenish the money, but the military got suspicious and refused to fund Quicksilver anymore."

"That's why we had to suddenly run Mercury. Until Janet took the money, Georgiana played along with the military so she could work on her projects," said Charlie. "But what was the deception?"

Sally finished her red wine before answering. "Apparently, a former vice president, who hated Canada, not so many years back sent five Navy destroyers to the Canadian Northwest Territories. He wanted to claim them as American since they were not that populated. The deception is that it did not happen, even though the Canadian Coast Guard had to pull the five destroyers out of the ice. I'm glad I'm not into deception. It seems ridiculous."

"I agree. But coming back to Janet, I can only imagine what relationship mother and daughter had after the company went bankrupt. Georgiana starts another company and Janet goes to jail," said Charlie.

"What is worse for Janet is that Jenkins will be a manager in Georgiana's new company, who has the same military contracts to keep the deception going. Jenkins said Georgiana plans to keep searching for a way to keep women from going through childbirth," said Sally.

A few weeks later, the deception was threatened when Janet's sentence was commuted for time served. She refused to go back to work for her mother and instead went to work for Marge Willywrighter and the Granite Company. It was a good way to get back at her mother, who would never know when her daughter would seek revenge.

Soon, Charlie's divorce became final thanks to a Florida streamlined process. Charlie celebrated by asking Sally to his house for dinner. His daughters were into cooking and he thought he would share the pain. Over the next few months, the dinner dates became more frequent, and Charlie hoped the dinners with Sally would one day become permanent.

Rebuilding Childhood and Looking for Home

At different times, I've known two women who were raped. Some of this story is fiction, but their reaction to the violence is true. I am disappointed I couldn't totally capture the women's emotions, but I wanted something. This is the best I could do.

The tall man grabbed Gwen where streetlights only brushed at the night's darkness. His right hand clamped onto her thin face and she struggled to breathe. His other hand wrapped around her small body like a vise and lifted her up and back.

She did not know what to do with her legs twisting in the air, but to kick wildly. As he threw her on the ground, dull ground objects dug into her back and grass tickled her neck. A knife appeared in one of his hands close to her nose. Yards away, cars and trucks swished by as Gwen worried about her daughter waiting to be picked up.

When Gwen was twelve-years-old, she had a lot to say about her approaching maturity. She tried talking to her girlfriends at school about her evolving life, but they had their own maturity to deal with. She talked to her mother, who would only discuss female hygiene as if talking about anything else meant feelings had to be exposed. There was no talking to her father about almost anything, since he seemed to resent her growing up, anyway.

To compensate for the lack of attention she received, Gwen recorded her maturing life in her diary. She did not want to forget who she was developing into during what she thought was an important year of her life.

Yet Gwen could not write about her best thoughts. They were too revealing to herself. Instead, she wrote about how it was to live in a rural post office area called Maria. A place consisting of a sawmill, a general store where the post office was kept, a used car lot, and eighty-two ranch style houses that bordered both sides of the narrow country road.

The sawmill employed most of the people, everyone bought their staples at the general store, and the used car lot sold cars and pickups so everyone had something to drive to the sawmill and general store. Most of the vehicles could not make it very far beyond those places.

What did make it out of Maria five days a week was a diesel locomotive and six flatbeds. Each morning as the train approached, the heavy rumble shook the ground and its horn blared once, long and slow. When she could, Gwen skipped breakfast and stood in the sawmill with the tall workmen before catching the school bus. She watched the powerful locomotive push in with long rows of hewed trees looking like corpses.

In the afternoon, the school bus dropped Gwen off at the sawmill to wait for her dad who worked there. As the train began to leave with cut lumber, she wanted to scream at the horn, which blew twice, for leaving her alone in a post office area not even significant enough to be called a town.

Gwen vowed she would leave Maria one day with its sawdust, mud, and empty roads. She wanted to live near people and have friends who were happier. She focused on school studies with the hopes of college. Except, she worried her plans were in jeopardy if she couldn't understand school math.

Confused one day by a particularly strong math lesson, in the evening after supper she asked her father for help. He sat at the kitchen table reading the morning paper as if the day had not happened.

"You write in your diary too much. It's taking away from your math studying. When I was your age my father made me keep an apology jar," he explained.

"Do you still have it?" Gwen knew nothing about her father's past. She asked him for help only because he was too smart to continue with school after his first year of high school.

"I kept the jar for my father and it doesn't matter whether it helped or not." He had a sadness in his voice, like a curse he was passing along. "It would make you feel better if you write an apology on a slip of paper and stuff it in a jar when you did something wrong," he said.

His voice carried unemotionally over Gwen's head as he went into the pantry and brought out a half-gallon jar. It used to hold pickled eggs. He handed it to Gwen, saying, "I've been saving this for you. Tape some green construction paper around the belly. You don't want anyone looking at your apologies."

"Who would I write the apology to?" Gwen asked, holding the large jar in her small hands. She twisted it around and nearly dropped it before her father took it away and placed it on a low pantry shelf.

"You'd write something and put it in the jar when you did wrong against a person." Gwen's father went back to the kitchen table and his paper.

"What if they did me wrong?" Gwen got confused.

"How can someone do you wrong? You're just a little girl. I'll make it easy on you. Me and your mother will tell you when to put an apology in the jar. After 'while, you'd understand what I'm talkin' about and you'd feel better," Gwen's father said, walking into the living room with his newspaper.

"Why would that make me feel better? And what did all this have to do with math?" Gwen asked, but not too loudly or else her father could come back with her first apology lesson. She stared at the open math book sitting on the kitchen table, wondering why her father explained apologies, but not math.

In time, the jar's small slips of paper became apologies to her parents for their criticism, teachers because Gwen could not understand math, classmates who did not include her at lunch, friends she did not have, and others she no longer wanted to remember. She never understood what lesson the jar was supposed to make, but it became filled with her best thoughts about her young, maturing life she had grown to dislike.

Over time, Gwen's father stopped paying attention to the apology jar, but her mother demanded more apologies. Her mother became obsessed with the jar. The more they did not talk to each other, the more they did not talk about their feelings, the more apologies Gwen had to write to satisfy her mother.

Gwen saw the jar as all the negatives in her life, and she saw no reward for any good she had done. The jar left her no time to write in her diary to explain who she was becoming. To Gwen, the jar became her motivation to one day leave the rural post office area of Maria.

Gwen ground her teeth in pain and pinched her fingernails into the man's shirt and flesh. She wanted to draw blood. She felt his labored, rapid breath catch on her face and neck. She wanted to dream away her life, but she had her little girl to think about.

Each summer growing up, Gwen listened to the music get faster, the boy's voices get deeper, and the girls' talk get chattier. At sixteen, her mother had lost interest in Gwen and the apology jar.

Also, Gwen decided there were too many apologies in the jar, although she knew there should have been more.

In late September after school started, Gwen went out at two in the morning to the small stream that created one of Maria's boundaries. Under a full moon, she broke open the jar with a river rock. Using the butt of her first cigarette, she burned the scraps of paper and sent them floating into the slow-moving dark stream.

The cigarette smoke rawed her throat and itched her eyes as moonlight danced across her face. Not long after that, she gave up the cigarettes and wished she had kept the scraps of paper. They could have helped her remember those important years of her young life.

That year as a sophomore, Gwen stuck on a little makeup each week until the boys talked to her in a different way. She was okay with that. Girls confided in her about boys. She was okay with that, too. Math was not important after all. In her final year of high school, Gwen got out of Maria and into college through a special graduation present from her father.

A week before graduation, he died when his heart exploded in his chest. It was like a murder without a murderer. He would never make it to foreman at the sawmill and Gwen's mother would never make it to the "somebody" role. But Gwen made it out of Maria with her share of the insurance money. Almost like her father had planned it that way.

The day after Gwen left for college, her mother sold the ancestral home to live with her older sister near Chesapeake Bay where trees were not as dense. Less than three months after Gwen's father died, all material items concerning a life with him had been sold, given away, or taken to the Salvation Army. He ceased to exist except in some photographs, a few mementos, and fading memories.

Gently, the rapist lessened his grip as if an uncontrollable seizure in him had subsided. Gwen had no control or desire to feel. She lost her sense of being.

In college, Gwen felt like she belonged. The campus sat nestled in the middle of a small mountain town and courses gave her a schedule to follow; so she knew where to go, what to do, and when. She evolved into someone less shy and wondered at what point she became a woman.

"Why don't you come live with me and finish your schooling here?" Gwen's mother kept asking.

"I like it here. I've got friends."

"You'll like yourself better here and maybe meet someone. Also, you can help me adjust to this life near the water."

"Being around you doesn't make me a better person. All I'll be is another of you," said Gwen.

"I should have had another child. Maybe the second one would have been a boy who loved his mother. I know you don't like yourself where you are."

"Because you don't like yourself there does not mean I don't like myself here."

The phone calls were like this until graduation. Her father had long since disappeared from their conversations, and Gwen grew to ignore her mother's complaints. Meeting Calvin in her senior year helped with the transition out of college.

A tiny marriage ceremony with a reception in a church basement led to a one-bedroom apartment in a crowded city between Maria and the college. School memories drifted away in the same direction as memories of her father and her childhood. After a few months as a wife, Gwen became pregnant.

Not until her third trimester did she see another woman look back at her from every mirror. Puzzled, Gwen did not know how she got to this point in her life so quickly. She wondered if her past ever existed and if memories were something to think about while falling into the future. Where was the now in all of this?

When Gwen gave birth to Cindy, the baby took her to another point beyond all that she knew before. Her daughter was someone to love and someone to love her. She wanted the best for her family and over the next two years Gwen slowly made the house into a home. The day she replaced the last Venetian blind with colorful print curtains, Calvin came home to announce he had met another woman.

"It just isn't working out between us, Gwen. It doesn't mean I don't love you, but we've grown apart," Calvin said. "I'm moving in with her."

"What do you mean 'grown apart'? We've only been married for two years and known each other for three. How can anyone grow apart in three years unless they're twelve years old?" Gwen said.

They stood in the kitchen of the completed house as Gwen moved her spinach casserole from the oven to the countertop with two pot holders that looked like fighting gloves.

"Listen to me while I tell you how things are going to be."

"Shut up. Why did you have to find somebody else? What's wrong with me? Hell, what's wrong with you?" Gwen's voice rose sharply, uncontrollably, and without direction or decision.

"I know it's going to be rough for a while, but... "

"What about Cindy? You're leaving her, too. Did you know that?"

"She's too little to understand. I'll be around when she's growing up. It won't be that bad." Calvin said as he looked at the casserole and not at Gwen.

"How will you be around when you're moving into your 'somebody else's' place? Look at this house. It's supposed to be our home."

"Don't start pleading with me, Gwen. It won't make it any easier and I won't feel sorry for you after I leave."

"I don't want you to feel sorry for me, ever. I can handle what you're doing to us." With a sweep of her arm, Gwen sent the casserole into the air toward Calvin. It crashed between them, mixing sharp pieces of porcelain with dark spinach leaves, chicken cubes, and her special mushroom sauce.

The loud, sudden sound woke Cindy, who cried in the next room. While Gwen went to her child, Calvin went out the door.

Alone the first night in the completed house, Gwen stared at the bland ceiling over her bed. Instead of being afraid, she let the knowledge of her two-year-old girl sleeping in the next bedroom become the only thing to think about.

The rape happened four months after the divorce in the interim period when Gwen ran late from her job and missed her bus. To make up for time and not leave Cindy in daycare any longer, she cut through a dimly lit path to the next street, hoping to catch the bus there.

Finished with his act of violence, the man walked away as if he had eaten a steak dinner. Gwen watched his silhouette against the streetlights and refused to be unimportant. She rose from the dirt like an eagle taking flight and ran after him, trying not to trip on her torn dress.

He ran into the busy street where a car whizzed between them. Gwen hesitated as another car zipped past her. In frustration, she clenched her fists and screamed. He missed a step, looking back at her scream.

Desperate sounds of squealing tires and a shrill car horn came with the image of metal on flesh. He went hurling across the black pavement. She watched him with emotional numbness.

At the trial, Gwen saw he would always be a paraplegic. As he was crippled physically, Gwen was crippled mentally. After the trial, Gwen took Cindy away to a Virginia 'burg to live in the basement of her grandparent's house, her father's parents.

"No, I won't live with you. You're too much like Calvin," Gwen told her mother before the move.

"It would have been worse if you married someone like your father," Mother struck back.

"If I marry again, it won't be like either of you." The rape challenged Gwen to dislike men in general and in total.

"I feel guilty about the rape," Calvin called Gwen on the drive to her grandparents.

She wanted to say that he should feel guilty since it was his divorce that put her in the situation to be raped. But she didn't see any need to nurse guilt and regret into their struggling relationship. It would only grow into a monster.

Ignoring his comment, Gwen said, "Give me a few days to settle in before we arrange visitation times with Cindy."

She needed time to understand how it would be to live with her father's parents. When they made the offer, Gwen wanted to get away from the place where the attack happened, and she needed a break from living alone.

At her grandparents, no one talked about the attack that brought her there. Everyone seemed to fear knowing the truth.

"Your father used to live here in the basement," Grandpa told Gwen after she had lived there a week. The place continued to smell musty, and Gwen was not curious to look for traces of her father.

"He got that job down south when jobs weren't much here. I told him to get back, but you're all that has ever returned."

Gwen continued to be quiet. She held Cindy's clothes, unsure where to put them. The basement space was too big with too much furniture. However, it would have been a good place for her dad to live in.

"I didn't favor your mother, his wife. She changed him into an indifferent man. He used to be more caring." He seemed to be talking to his son's ghost.

"Dad said you made him keep an apology jar. Why?"

"He fell off his bike when he was small and hurt his head. After that, he had trouble concentrating and adjusting to people. I thought if he wrote down his apologies and put them in a jar, he would think about things more carefully and have friends. I realized too late that it made him worse. Before I could tell him I was wrong, he quit his first year of high school and found work at a retail store where he met your mother. She convinced him to leave. I should have told him to keep a diary. He wouldn't have destroyed that." Gwen's grandpa walked away with his regrets hanging in the basement air.

The next week, Gwen told the stylist to keep cutting until there was just enough to cover her scalp. She threw out her makeup, except for the lipstick, and wore more leather and brown cotton in contrast to the bright colors and complicated patterns of her previous clothes. The mold of her figure disappeared in bulky layers. Yet, underneath she wore feminine, silky underwear that felt tight and lacy.

Gwen liked to get makeovers in the cosmetic section of high-priced department stores. While her grandparents took care of Cindy, makeup artists had opinions about where the rouge should be placed, the shade of lipstick Gwen could use, and what eyeshadow hue went with the facial mix. She went home and washed it all away, even throwing away what she had bought. Gwen felt like a Dr. Jekyll and Mr. Hyde.

When Gwen and Cindy were not in the basement, Grandma came down to wash clothes that had been worn more than once. Gwen hated who she had become, having someone help her cope. After three weeks, she found part-time work in a women's clothing store she could walk to.

Her grandparents watched Cindy and one afternoon Gwen came into the kitchen where her grandpa was making cookies with Cindy. Gwen wondered if they would be edible with the mustard, ketchup, and chocolate chip mix.

"You have plans for your future?" Grandpa asked after Grandma came into the kitchen, saw the mess her husband had made, and walked back out muttering he had to clean things up.

"I'm working on it."

"You can't let the past cause you to avoid the future," he said.

"I'll think about it. First we need to see how these cookies taste," said Gwen.

It was a test of wills for each of them to eat one. They left the rest for the garbage man to carry away. Cindy enjoyed the cookie making so much that Grandpa agreed to try it again soon.

Grandpa ran outside with Cindy to show her the first stars as they appeared. Grandma came to help with the kitchen mess. Both women settled into discussing anything besides the future. They all seemed content for nothing to happen.

A lot happened two days later when a letter came from the rapist.

It arrived in a franked envelope with too much postage. On thin paper, his typed words tried to explain what made him do it, like an apology. The letter's abrupt shortness left Gwen without a purpose for the communication. She did not understand his "I'm sorry" statement before his signature. It looked like a postscript, an afterthought.

Gwen did not know the motivation behind the letter and she did not want to know. Reading it made her numb and tired. How could he be sorry? Maybe he was sorry since he was helpless the rest of his life. Maybe he knew how I felt lying helpless on my back, she thought.

Putting the letter back into the envelope, Gwen wondered how much of what he said she assumed he should have said. She did not want to read the letter again.

The envelope sat on Gwen's dresser where Cindy could not reach it. It became like a taboo her grandma avoided when she cleaned the room. Three days after its arrival and at two in the morning, Gwen sat on the back porch with a full moon hanging above the horizon.

She used a wooden match to touch the edges of the letter and watched the paper shrivel on the concrete patio. Like the apology jar from her childhood, Gwen burned the apology from her rapist and continued to erase her past as best she could.

Back in the basement with Cindy asleep, Gwen pulled out her long forgotten diary. It had blank pages. She began writing as if filled with a fever. But not about her thoughts. They were in a mess.

She wrote children's stories about the robins and blue jays fighting in the backyard trees. She wrote about the family of groundhogs living beneath the rotting timbers of an old house down the street. In literary form, she described how an elderly lady passed their house every day in a stiff walking stance without ever saying a word and never turning her head. Gwen wrote about how much she always wanted to be far away, riding on a train across long distances to places she had read about in travel blogs.

By the next evening, she filled the diary and continued her words in a notebook her grandpa brought her. Over the next few days, her grandma brought her simple meals. Grandpa brought her more notebooks.

Each night she wrote more, read a few lines to her daughter, and passed some pages onto her grandparents. Soon, Gwen moved her pages from the desk to the refrigerator for security. Her descriptions drew boundaries around her life. Her writing took form.

The more she wrote, the less Gwen raised her voice to Cindy and her grandparents. She thought about her future and she let the past be a memory she wrote in her notebook.

On the first warm spring day, Gwen took Cindy to River Park. They walked slowly across a wide pasture where young adults tossed frisbees, children ran in circles around themselves, and career men and women took off their shoes to walk in the soft grass. Across this pasture and through a thin line of trees, Gwen found a sandy spot by the wide, slow-moving river.

Mother and daughter sat on the coarse sand with a light breeze off the warm water touching their faces. In the distance came the sound of a train horn tooting twice.

Gwen and Cindy talked incessantly about nothing in particular. Cindy, who did not cry as much anymore, built shapes in the sand with her mother. When the shapes crumbled, they built them again.

Comics Have It All

I am not a comedian. But I struggle to see red and green. I wish the world had more blue and yellow.

It's Comedy Man! With his wonderful cotton shirt of azure blue and flannel trousers of marvelous chartreuse yellow. These colors made him a happy person on stage. Except he did not think his audience understood his happiness.

They laughed before his joke's big reveal or when he did not have a punchline during his anti-jokes. He pondered this calamity and hoped he understood comedy. So, he gave in to their off-laughter. On his neck he wore a woolen scarf of lizard green and a long silk tie of burning red.

Comedy Man worried the audience would be happy with his greens and reds and not his blues and yellows. He tried to explain to them, as they waited for a reason to laugh, that he had a blindness to reds and greens. He saw a vacant look of comedy in those colors.

The audience laughed. Just look, they cried out. The colors are right there on you. So, he told them his joke.

"I saw a tin can painted a colorless gray. I pretended the can had rainbow colors. Don't tell the tin can." On stage, the audience laughed at his gray joke. It made the funny meter when heard rather than read.

Off stage preparing for his comedic routine, he pinned on his chest bachelor buttons since he lacked a companion in life. On his ankle, blue bells helped him put a dance in his step while yellow roses stuck out of his lapel for show. To keep something for himself, he kept bull thistle in his pants back pocket and lanceleaf coreopsis (who were really tickseed) protected in his front pants pocket. Woodland sunflower, safely tucked in his shirt pocket, could one day be seven feet high.

All these kept Comedy Man's spirits comedic and happy amid the greens and reds the audience wore. Colors he could not see that well. He had to try harder with his comedy when he did not match the colors of the audience.

In his dressing room before another show, Comedy Man struggled with how to be funny. On his vanity, he kept camphor-weed (bad tasting), Black-Eyed Susan (who got hit by the large softball), and purple trillium erectum (always in waiting and wanting). Next to his makeup mirror he rested some marsh skullcap that he wore when he felt silly, blue curl flowers to stop deathly silliness, and St. John's Wort he should take a lot more of. No matter what was around him, Comedy Man knew the audience wanted those *other* colors.

He went on stage and announced, "My comedic anchors are blues and yellows. These colors make me laugh correctly." The audience stared at him and he stared back and all the staring made him think he could be wrong and they could be right. Particularly when there was not much laughter during his comedy routine.

Another show in front of another audience, Comedy Man brought on stage a black suitcase. From it he lifted out blue wild-flower delphiniums that grew tall and needed support, like he needed sometimes standing in front of an unlaughing audience. He took out love-in-a-mist with their whimsical blue blooms and true-blue flower hydrangeas, both giving him hope for true love one day. He pulled out blue daisies that bees and butterflies loved. Whatever they loved, he loved.

Next came yellow marigolds with layers of ruffled petals like a flowered dress, daffodils with trumpet-like yellow structures announcing friends he wished he had, and goldenrod with tall leafy stalks streaking toward the ceiling as if they were outside in the sun.

He let the flowers fall onto the stage at his feet. With each dropped flower, he added a topper with running gags. He switched a story to make a joke, putting the last line of a joke first, and kept a joke going when the audience thought it ended. Each time, he recited jokes with a punch line filled with funny "K's" that helped with the unexpected (no surprise, no laugh).

Wearing their greens and reds, the audience hit Comedy Man with laughter at his jokes and gags as he discarded the blues and yellows at his feet. Looking down at his flowers, he survived his performance.

This had become Comedy Man's lot in life. Trying to make laugh and merriment and glad feelings while competing with greens and reds that, to him, represented sadness. He imagined these were the colors of the world's news and political agendas. They represented dark personages of newscasters and politicians who talked ugly opinions and promoted fear with torrid sexual drama.

This was his competition. The uncomedic story of violence in a world colored in greens and reds. Yet, he persisted in trying to be funny with his blues and yellows.

"Here I come," said Comedy Man before yet another crowd of sullen faces. They stared at him through the spotlights, giving him a "you're on" attitude. He looked out at the audience he assumed wore greens and reds. There were even browns he could not distinguish if they were really browns, greens, or reds. These colors reflected upward to the cathedral ceilings that held decay written in the mold.

With this performance, Comedy Man carried two one-gallon paint cans onto the stage. He shuddered with a tenseness in his face, a tingle in his hands, and a tautness in his legs as he stood straight and tall. Comedy Man was ready for this performance. He was not holding back.

In his most practiced acrobatic move, he twirled, spun, and jumped mostly in the same spot. When he landed, Comedy Man pressed a lever and a gush of compressed air propelled each of the can's contents out toward the audience. In a hurricane-like, tornado-turning pop, two clouds of blue and yellow shredded paper flew into the air over the audience's upturned faces. In midair, the shredded paper fell toward the people waiting to laugh.

Except this did not happen. Some manufactured wind, some cooling air to maintain temperature, stilled Comedy Man's performance. His shredded paper hung inside the sky of the small auditorium as if looking for redemption. The crowd gasped, wearing their greens and reds as the blues and yellows floated over their frowns like a cloud of hope.

Desperate, Comedy Man threw into the audience the bachelor buttons he wore. He pulled the blue bells off his ankles and yellow roses off his lapel. The blue thistle and lanceleaf coreopsis came out next, followed by the woodland sunflower.

People in the audience caught the flowers and smiled. More people cheered at the disposal of his flowers while the shredded paper of colors over their heads spun around as if laughing at Comedy Man. The audience could not hold back what was wanted in surprise.

The audience threw anything green and red up into the air just far enough for the shredded blues and yellows to come down. A clash of colors peppered everyone with the possibility of colorful, happy lives and good endings. The audience tossed the blues and yellows, greens and reds back into the air, then again and again. Who pays attention to a comedian at this point?

Comedy Man laughed. A laughter like Abbott and Costello or Laurel and Hardy. The crowd laughed like Sinbad or Carol Burnett. Everyone laughed like a Laugh-In *Let's Go To The Party* episode.

Comedy Man did not have the talents of these other comedians. Yet, there he stood before an audience who raised their hands toward the ceiling, laughing and wanting more. They hoped to keep their laughter from being washed away by the pain held in the narrow, violent world they lived in just outside the moldy plaster walls.

Doing a Jack Benny and breaking the fourth wall where stage characters talked to the audience, Comedy Man gave the best performance of his long career. Laughter united the colors together. There was singing and hugging, dancing and clapping.

Yet all things end. The laughter faded, the colors became gray, and everything stopped quick and hurried-like as if a clock somewhere said so. Everyone went home to watch hate filled news and listen to meaningless political banter and wait for the next time they had enough and needed to feel happy.

After the show, Comedy Man rode a city bus populated with working men and women who had worked too many hours. It was in the early morning, long before daybreak, when he looked at these people and considered the possibility he could be a laughable person who had nothing to laugh about. Will the news and politics of the world one day stop people from laughing? This was his biggest worry.

Sitting on a torn seat, he told himself, "Tomorrow I'll try black and white balloons. Inside each, I'll put the seed of a flower. I'll sing jokes to the audience as the balloons float to the ceiling where the hot lights will pop them open and give the audience something to plant. No one will know if the flower will be blue, yellow, green, or red when it sprouts and grows."

When he got to his one-bedroom apartment, Comedy Man struggled to find his happiness. He gulped merlot straight out of the bottle and wished he could see more color. In his faux leather recliner, the TV images before him revealed a violent world with no happiness or color.

"Maybe my talent is reserved for those living in gray," he told the bottle of merlot.

In his recliner, Comedy Man drifted off to sleep. Soon, Buster Keaton and Lucille Ball took his hand and led him away while thanking Comedy Man for trying so hard to have color in his comedic life.

The Decision

When I was in college (night school), I wrote an essay about euthanasia for a class assignment. At the same time, a co-worker found out he had cancer, went home, and hung himself.

"Do you think God will forgive me?"

Inside the confessional and through the small latticed window, Father Horatio said nothing.

"Am I talking to God when I talk to you?" Tommy thought the hard wooden seats were too uncomfortable to stay sitting in for long. Suppose a person had a lot of things to confess?

"When I received my Holy Orders and was ordained as a priest, I became one who acts in the power of Christ." Father Horatio sounded unsure.

Tommy was unsure why his priest had to explain his ordination. It didn't answer the question. Before he could ask again, Father Horatio asked, "Do you think the doctors are right?"

"I had three opinions and way too many tests to prove their opinions are not opinions, but facts."

Tommy wondered if the confessional had all this flimsy wooden structure so there would not be any echoes. A person hearing echoes might mistake that for God talking to them.

"I cannot approve of this," said the priest.

"I'm not asking *you* to approve anything. I'm asking if God would forgive me." Peering into the small latticed square window they spoke through, Tommy saw Father Horatio squirm in his seat.

Silence again. Tommy thought maybe the priest's butt was sore from sitting on a hard wooden seat. Tommy's certainly was, and he hadn't been sitting that long. He leaned again to look through the square window and couldn't see any movement. They need more lighting in these places, he thought as he wondered why they had to have a partition. They both knew each other.

To break the silence, Tommy explained, "I don't hurt, yet. Actually, I feel pretty good for someone with less than six months to live."

"Can't they cure you? Can't they kill this thing that's in you?"

Tommy thought a priest should not be talking about killing. "No cure unless they kill me and the cancer is doing that already. I'm okay with everything because I don't think of death as an ending. It's more like a crossing over to something that tastes better. I'm hoping it tastes like buttered pasta and warm, soft bread with a slice of cherry pie."

"So, you want God to forgive you for killing yourself."

"To be clear, I'm killing myself so I can donate my body parts before they get contaminated with the cancer. Also, I'm only cheating God by six months when I'll be dead, anyway."

"All I can say is it's a sin to commit suicide." Father Horatio sounded unconvincing.

"Yeah, well it's also against the law." Tommy heard the wooden bench creak as the priest stood up and pushed open the thin door to exit the confessional. Tommy thought he was coming around to his side. Instead, he heard Father Horatio's hard-sole shoes bang against the solid flooring of the church as he walked away. Maybe he went to the altar looking for guidance from God, Tommy thought. Or maybe he had to pee.

Waiting for his priest to come back, Tommy thought he could take a nap if the seat was not made of wood and too hard to sleep on. He waited five minutes, but Father Horatio did not come back.

"Maybe he's using his rosary to check with the head angel Michael. That rosary had a lot of beads to pray through," Tommy muttered to the stale air within the small wooden enclosure.

The dark wood did not answer back. After another few minutes, Tommy became too uncomfortable to sit any longer and he pushed open the thin paneled door and left. He was used to people running away from him when he talked about his coming death. But he didn't think his priest would run.

Walking out of the church into the humid summer air, Tommy thought about the cancer he had. It was like a special friend who could not control himself. Someone who was becoming unmanageable and difficult to ignore or understand or forget.

On the way to his car, Tommy whispered to the thing growing inside him, "I cannot love you with all this hate I have for you. But I'll make sure we die in peace." Tommy thought this sounded too much like a Faulkner story. But he didn't care.

He passed healthier people who would die one day, too. At least I know what I'll die of, he wanted to shout at them. They kept walking past him and he kept walking toward his death.

Tommy drove home to his wife Sally, who he found in the living room staring at the same romance book as when he left her over an hour ago.

"I think you should keep working as long as you can. It'll give me more money to pay down this mortgage." Sally hissed at him as he stepped into the one-bedroom condo they invested in a year ago.

"Buying this place was your idea. Why don't you sell it?" Tommy walked into the kitchen, which took two steps.

"I'd have to sell it at a loss."

"I'm losing my life."

"I don't understand why you're doing this? What will people say about me? Besides, it's against the law." Sally shouted into her romance book. She slammed the book closed, staring at the carpet before her.

"I'm hoping to help at least one person with my body parts." He opened the refrigerator and got out a stout beer.

"Why don't you let the cancer kill you like normal people?" Sally crossed and recrossed her legs. She did not look at Tommy.

"I was never a normal person. Even when I married you."

"This is not a joke. Yeah, you'll be dead, but I'll have to live with what you did. You're not going to do this to me."

Since this morning's argument when he told her of his intentions, Tommy had given up getting his wife to understand that he was the one dying.

Sally stood up and threw her romance book on the floor between them. She glared at her husband. Sometimes a one-bedroom condo did not provide enough room for two people, Tommy thought as he guzzled his beer and stared back.

"I hate you. I won't get any insurance money when you die like this. If you let the cancer kill you, I'll get paid something for your death."

Tommy couldn't help getting angry. "I don't give a crap about you anymore. There are wives and husbands somewhere who would support someone like me. They'd be proud that I would do this to help people."

"Hey, wait a minute. That's really why you're doing this, isn't it? You don't care about helping other people. You're afraid of the pain and suffering and you want people to think you're a hero instead of a coward," Sally said with a one-sided smirk.

Clenching his teeth, Tommy was determined to control his anger. "Yeah, I wanted people to see me as some type of hero instead of a sickly man who needed help peeing. But then I thought about how scary it was to kill myself. It's scarier than having the cancer. And you know what? I'm scared about all of this and I no longer care about heroes or what anyone would think of me. I haven't done anything in my life to really help anyone. This is my last chance to do something good and I hope God understands that."

Tommy got another beer and flipped on the TV, trying to control his anger. He found the Catholic channel where a priest talked of divine forgiveness for anyone who was Catholic. Tommy changed the channel and watched the Baptist station where the preacher yelled about how people were going to hell for watching TV, even if it was the Baptist station. To save themselves, they had to send a donation.

Tommy turned the TV off. "I talked to our priest."

"God's not going to save you. Even if you talked to Father Horatio." Sally sat down and went back to her romance book like it would save her.

Before they were married, Tommy thought about how he used to like Sally's voice. He finished his beer.

"You want to say goodbye?" Tommy approached the front door.

"What! You're not doing it today, are you? You can't. It's not a good day for me. I need to get myself ready mentally. Why don't you listen to me? Why can't you work at least another month or two? That'll give me more money to live on." Sally stared at her paperback.

Tommy couldn't see her face. He considered going to her and offering his hand in sympathy, pleading with her to not worry about him. But he finally accepted that she only cared about herself.

"I have a few days of vacation time saved up. You should get that money. Also, since I'm donating my body parts, you won't have to pay for a funeral," said Tommy.

Sally looked up from her romance book. "I have no intention of paying for your funeral. That's your problem."

Tommy hated romance books. They were so much like fiction. "You want to be there when I do it?"

She gave him a look of absolute horror that transitioned to disgust, the ugly kind. Finally, she formed some version of rage Tommy was unsure of.

"OK, so you're not going to be there. You want to say goodbye?"

"I'm warning you. Don't you kill yourself today. I'm not ready for it." Sally flipped a page, ripping it out of the book. "I'll call the police."

"I'll just get out and do it, anyway."

"I could kill you for trying to kill yourself and leaving me like this." Sally gripped the book like she would throw it at him.

Tommy stomped out of the condo. He did not say goodbye as Sally returned to her romance book that was missing a page.

In his car, Tommy felt guilty about leaving his wife like that. They had been married two years after dating for a year and he planned on a future together. But as medical people each time confirmed his diagnosis, she stopped coming with him to the appointments or talk about his cancer.

Like it was my fault I got the cancer that had no cure, he thought. Stopped at a traffic light, Tommy realized that his death was getting easier to realize. The light turned green.

After an hour of driving around making connections with the last people he would make connections with, Tommy came to his favorite bar. A chic, trendy place where people enjoyed sitting in private booths and he could sit alone at the long polished bar. He watched himself in the massive bar mirror drink dark beer and red wine. He was on his third beer and second wine when Father Horatio sat down beside him.

They stared at each other's reflection in the mirror. Tommy waved to the bartender for another draft beer and a glass of wine that he brought too fast. The priest's clerical white collar seemed to intimidate the bartender.

"Sally wanted me to talk to you. She said I'd find you here. Are you really going to do it today?" Father Horatio turned to look at Tommy.

"At sunset."

"Can't you wait?"

"Why wait? The cancer is not waiting. It keeps growing."

Father Horatio drank the wine and Tommy the beer. When these were empty, Tommy ordered more. The bartender was ready for them.

"You asked me if God would forgive you. If I told you God wouldn't, would you still commit this act?" Father Horatio stared into his dark wine.

"I decided I'll talk to God about all of this when I get there, wherever there is," said Tommy, drinking his draft beer.

"I want to know about it." Father Horatio finished his glass of wine in three gulps.

"How to kill yourself?" Tommy finished his beer.

"How to think yourself dead." Father Horatio sounded like he was giving a sermon he didn't want to give.

"It's going to be hard to do this, but the cancer is a great motivation. Besides, I believe the other side of life has to be all right since everybody ends up there, eventually."

"Based on your logic, everyone should commit suicide to save others. If everyone did that, there wouldn't be anyone to save." Father Horatio stared at Tommy's reflection in the bar mirror.

"That's not my logic, that's your illogic. Are you worried that God will blame you for not stopping me?"

Father Horatio stared into his empty glass. "I've made too many mistakes as a priest. I figured God is already overwhelmed with worry about me. With you, I want to understand your death and selflessness. It might help me."

The bartender brought them more beer and wine. This time, the priest drank the beer and Tommy the red wine.

After a few moments, Father Horatio looked at Tommy's reflection and said, "I want to be there when you do it. It'll help me decide where my faith is. Listening to people's confessions each day has been difficult for me lately and I don't trust my loyalty to keep doing it."

"And watching me die would help with all of this? Maybe you could get some cushions for the confessional and make it more comfortable."

Father Horatio did not smile. "I don't listen to confessions anymore. Yeah, I sit there with the confessors, but I sometimes forget people are even talking. They don't need me, anyway. They know what they did wrong."

Tommy asked, "Why do you continue to be a priest?"

"When I entered my vocational discernment to prepare for my candidacy of priesthood, I don't think I vacated all of my vices. It is causing me to question my faith."

"Like what vices?"

"I've never seen someone die."

"Haven't you ever given someone their last rites?"

"There are no last rites. It's called the Sacrament of the Anointing of the Sick and is used for people in grave conditions or about to have a serious operation. It's for the remission of sins, giving of spiritual strength, and to have good health."

"One of those 'grave conditions' had to be someone dying."

"I ran away before they died."

"Like you did in the confessional."

"I do that sometimes with other people, too. They sound like they're dying when they confess." Father Horatio did not sound regretful.

"Are you going to give me the Sacrament?"

"I give it to anyone requesting it. Since you're doing suicide, I recommend you get it. The Sacrament is supposed to give you fortitude when facing death, a union with the Passion of Christ, and to prepare you to meet God in hope rather than in fear."

"I could use that hope," said Tommy.

Father Horatio gulped down his beer and Tommy finished his wine. They both turned on their barstools to look at each other. Tommy wondered if he should order more drinks, but Father Horatio turned his glass upside down on the counter.

"The Sacraments are also supposed to restore your health, but I think you're beyond that," he said.

Tommy threw three one-hundred-dollar bills on the counter for payment. "That's one for each of the Trinity. All right, let's go see me die."

They came to an empty dirt lot next to the hospital parking. Not even weeds grew out of the hard, desolate soil. The sun had set and where they stood was not too dark because of the nearby hospital lights. But dark enough that no one would notice two men standing in a vacant dirt lot. A full moon glared down at them.

Father Horatio spoke first. "I thought I could help people find hope if I became a priest. After six years of seminary school, I was ordained to the Diaconate as a transitional deacon. Yet, something was missing and that was death. I need to know about death before I continue with this priest thing."

"Wouldn't it be easier to go to that hospital? I'm sure someone is dying there," said Tommy.

"I don't like hospitals. Too many germs. I could catch something and die."

Tommy waited for Father Horatio to explain more. But the priest stared at Tommy waiting for him to do something. With nothing changing in their surroundings, Tommy decided to go ahead with his dying.

"The drugs I take won't hurt my organs. As I die, I'll push a pre-set button on my smartphone and notify a group of doctors and nurses in that hospital where to find me. I already told them what I was doing and signed all the necessary papers. I didn't tell them when or where so they wouldn't get into trouble and be accused of assisted suicide. Hopefully, the police won't accuse you since you are just giving me my last rites. I mean Sacraments."

"What if they take your body parts before you're dead?"

"I don't care. At this point, I'm headed to another place outside of this life."

"You mean heaven." Father Horatio shivered in the warm air.

"You haven't given me the Sacraments yet and forgiven me for what I'm going to do." Tommy looked at the priest, who zipped open his bag.

Tommy sat down in the clay dirt as Father Horatio dug out a small jar.

"What's in the jar? I don't want you to give me something that will knock me out and stop me," said Tommy.

"This is olive oil for the anointing. My bishop blessed it. If you're allergic to olive oil, I have vegetable oil. They both work."

Tommy looked at the priest. "No, I'm not allergic to olive oil."

Father Horatio kneeled beside Tommy and made the sign of the cross on his forehead with the oil. Tommy thought it smelled pretty good. Reminded him of pasta and warm bread.

"Through this holy anointing, may the Lord in his love and mercy help you with the grace of the Holy Spirit. May the Lord who frees you from sin save you and raise you up." The priest made more signs of the cross, just to be sure, probably. He stood up. "The Church recommends the Sacrament take place during Mass, but you probably don't want to wait until then."

With practiced movement, Tommy pulled out a long needle from his jacket pocket and jabbed it into his abdomen. In seconds, his eyes rolled upward and he flopped backward onto the ground.

"Wait a minute. Is that it?" Father Horatio grabbed for the needle, but it had already fallen on the ground, empty.

"Wait for it," whispered Tommy. He closed his eyes. In his left hand, he pushed a button on his smartphone.

Over the next few minutes, Father Horatio watched Tommy's breathing become shallow and ragged. The priest heard a low rattle form in Tommy's chest like a long-distance runner heading for the finish line. He smelled Tommy's last meal empty onto the ground.

Looking up, the Father Horatio saw people in white and blue coats run toward them. He held Tommy's hand as it relaxed like he was going to sleep. Father Horatio felt the energy of Tommy's soul depart his body, leaving it for the medical staff to help others.

Gabriel and The Blind Man

I read an article about a baseball player who became blind after a fastball struck him during a game. He said what saved him afterward from depression was his teddy bear that he kept since he was a child.

After the accident two years ago that made Peter blind, therapy people encouraged him to make friends as a support system. He never had friends when he could see, so he didn't see any reason to have friends when he couldn't see them.

To keep people away, Peter promoted an arrogant attitude toward anyone approaching him. It was his only talent left after becoming blind. Besides, I don't need a support system, he used to tell himself. Until recently.

He was losing hope that, despite some of his eyesight returning, the IRS still gave him a tax break for being a visually impaired person. Now, that arrogant talent seemed like nonsense and left him at thirty years old with no friends as a support system. Also, with no consistent employment.

He wanted a job like the one he had before his accident. However, that work required good eyesight that he no longer possessed. Instead, he found employers either feeling sorry for him or needing to fill their disability requirements. Eventually, he no longer wanted to be employed for his disability and quit. This followed quickly with a landlord who liked getting rent money.

This morning was time for Peter to move again. "It doesn't matter, Gabriel. We have experience relearning new surroundings. We'll find a new home, a new job, and a new life. Again."

Peter picked up his teddy bear and cradled it in his left arm. Gabriel understood him more than people he could smell, but not see.

Putting on jeans and a soft shirt that could be any color he imagined it to be, Peter followed the beads of Braille on an official document. He told Gabriel, "The policy makers beckon me south, where they plan to install me in a feel-good social program. Are you ready to leave this 'burg and find another?"

Before leaving, Peter found his pint of whiskey and swallowed what was left from the night before. "Now I'm ready for our journey."

Leaving his apartment, Peter told his teddy bear Gabriel, "Our word for today will be *gorgeous*. I know it will make me feel better no matter what happens."

On the sidewalk, he bumped into strangers who were not gorgeous with their comments. He had vehicles honk at him as he crossed streets he thought were sidewalks. He wished he could see sidewalks and streets better. They sometimes looked the same.

When he needed directions, he yelled out in frustration with the address. Someone always helped. Except he hated asking for help and he pushed the helper off or waved them to leave him alone. As they stomped away, he yelled that they were gorgeous for helping him. Peter wished he had grown up to be someone less like he was.

Eventually, he found a set of hard steps leading up to a harder platform. By the advice of soon-to-be train passengers, Peter kept back from the edge of the platform where only steel train tracks would catch his fall. He knew these passengers didn't care about him. If he fell, their train would be late getting his body off the tracks.

The engine rushed past Peter as he protected Gabriel from the heavy noise and odor of soot and diesel. He found metal stairs into the train car by smelling the sweaty people before him. Eventually, he found a dual seat that did not have the smell of another person in either seat.

The doors sealed everyone inside with drafts of manufactured air, pushing human odors and stale breaths around. Peter liked to think that sharing smells made them a family. Sitting on the window seat, he looked out the there was something to see.

"We're on our way. Everything is gorgeous," Peter told Gabriel, holding his teddy bear in his lap.

Except the train ride was taking too long and gave Peter time to think about the years before the accident. "I was a good short-stop, Gabriel. If it hadn't been for my accident, I would have moved up from that double AA team to the majors before the season ended."

Gabriel offered soft teddiness in sympathy. Peter accepted the softness, which helped him not get too deep in the emptiness he had coming over him.

Peter listened to the train's steel wheels sing as they traveled over the steel tracks. He said to Gabriel, "Everything will be alright. It's gorgeous to be on this adventure." Peter wished for no more adventures. He wanted to settle in one place and stop hoping one day to see.

"You're talking to yourself. Do you want something?" A woman's breathy voice tip-toed in his direction. She smelled like a person who wanted to be strong and sing.

"No, I don't need anything," Peter said. Except he wanted to see again.

"Everyone on this train is playing with their electronic gadgets. I swear some of them act like they're having sex with their video screens."

Peter felt the seat beside him drop, relaxing from someone's butt, hips, and legs settling into a sitting position next to him. She felt just as tall as he and warm.

She said, "Games and social media followers are like drug addicts. They can't look away."

"I can't see video screens, so it's easy for me," Peter said.

"I watched you get on the train and saw you can't see. You're a better person than me traveling around when you can't see good. I'd be a wreck."

"I manage. I don't want to talk about my blurry grayness that is neither exciting nor useful," said Peter.

"Sure, sure. I understand. We're about the same age," she said, as if being born in the same year meant they shared something.

Peter felt the train slow down. "Where are we?"

"We're almost to Richmond," said the woman. She had a husky accent banging inside her words.

"That sounds gorgeous."

"Some parts of the city may be gorgeous," she said cautiously.

"*Gorgeous* is my word for the day."

"Okay, now I get it. It's a great word. It makes me feel better already," she said, smelling like tears.

"I don't know what you look like, but I'm sure you look gorgeous." Peter said this to avoid an arrogant comment that would have sent this woman away. He was trying.

He felt her slender, warm hand collapse around his and lead his hand toward her face. She left it there for him to explore.

Peter slid his fingers up the slope of her soft forehead and deep into her thick, coarse hair. He wondered what color it was. His hand slipped down her delicate temple, under her small cheekbones, and slowly below her firm jaw. Strong features all of them, he thought.

She kept still as his hand came up to her round chin and gently pushed on her parted lips. They felt thick and he squished them together into a pucker that made her chuckle. Peter brought his hand back into his lap, happy with touching a human face that was not his own.

"Where are you going?" She asked as the train slowed down more.

"Wherever Gabriel takes me. It's always Gabriel who gets me home." Peter cuddled his teddy friend close to him.

"I guess Gabriel is that brown teddy?"

"His eyes get black when we go on a trip. When we get there, I decide he's looking through blue ones and he is a green teddy. I don't see either, but I take part in his excitement."

"I have some excitement," the woman said with a lack of excitement.

Peter waited for her to say more and wondered if she was crying. "Your voice means it is not a good excitement."

"Time's running out for me. I'm going to a hospital 'cause I got cancer," the voice of full lips said. "I've been sitting across the aisle from you and I decided that, when I die, you can have my eyes."

"Gorgeous."

"'Cause I'm givin' you my eyes?"

"It's your charity that's gorgeous. My eyes are fine. It's the connection with my brain and eyes that don't work right."

"I don't understand." She possessed a shaky tremble in her voice, like an emotion wanting to exhale.

"My brain was injured and my eyes rebelled, so the two are not talking to each other. In other words, my brain can't find what my eyes see. I would need your brain to see and that is like moving in together. We just met. But your offer is gorgeous."

Peter felt her stroking Gabriel, maybe for courage.

"Listen, I'm worried sick that my death is gonna be slow and painful. I can almost feel the cancer eatin' away at my insides right now. I'm gonna consider your word gorgeous as I die. But I agree you can't have my brain. I never got along that well with men. So, where ya goin' from here?"

"My social director suggested I start a new life at a job expo in a different city. I get aggravated at people giving me sympathy."

"Don't worry, I'm not givin' you no sympathy. Sympathy leads to pity and ends with regrets. I sometimes think I got too much pity in my head and that sympathy is also there screwin' 'round in my head leaving me with regrets."

He tried to understand the philosophy of this woman and thought he needed to know her name to help. "I'm Peter. This is Gabriel. And you are?"

"I'm scared. This cancer is like I was on death row and seeing the hangman's noose outside my cell block window."

"I don't like you being scared. It conflicts with my *gorgeous*. I'm going with you. Maybe the hospital has a job I can do. Like taking care of you."

"I don't want you going with me. Remember the pity and sympathy thing?"

"Let me feel your face again," said Peter.

"You felt enough. You comin' on to me? I'm in no good mood. I'm a dyin' woman."

"I'm a blind man."

"How did you get blind?"

"Let me feel your face, first."

Peter encountered a moment of silence as a drift of body heat moved toward him. Unexpectedly, the warm breath of the woman entered near his nose and mouth. He raised his hand cautiously and tapped her chin. "You're too close," he whispered.

She kissed him by sliding her soft, thick lips slowly across his. Her pressure smashed his mouth apart and swallowed his gasp. For a moment, he felt lost and wondered if he was still on the train. His senses were consumed and too quickly left starving as she pulled away, leaving his lips moist from her breath. He slipped open his eyes, trying to see where she went.

"I've never known a man who'd follow me to death. I'm getting off the train at Staples Mill. I looked at your papers and your stop is the one after mine at Main Street Station."

Somehow, Peter's other senses had failed to feel the motion of the train become motionless. He could smell her absence when he wanted her presence. "Damn glad she's gone, Gabriel," he lied.

Gabriel told him to stop torturing himself. When the train started moving again, Peter hated the woman for not saying her name. He wished he could see enough to follow her off.

At the next stop, Peter walked with long strides down city sidewalks, yelling his destination impatiently and shouting in frustration for directions. A few people shouted back and some tried to guide him along by following close next to him. He told them to go away. They were not the woman on the train.

At a street corner where people stood in his way, he cleared a path by swiping his cane back and forth across ankles. Ignoring the harsh complaints, he crossed the street, trusting one of those people he hit to tell him it was safe.

After a symphony of screeching tires and loud horns, Peter stumbled onto the opposing street corner where he found a double door. Inside, a woman greeter explained the event and that he had been listed as arriving. To Peter, it sounded like a sentencing.

He sat in one of the lobby's cushioned chairs, listening to the buzz of ongoing job interviews seep through nearby open conference room doors. However, Peter's listening attention became dragged toward a baseball game on the lobby's TV near him.

"Coming up to bat is Rodriquez, switch hitter for the visiting team," announced a man's elevated, squawky voice.

"It looks like the pitcher, Henderson, is ready for this one. No need to think about the pitch. And...strike one." This announcer sounded bored.

"These two have met before and there's always heat when the ball is singing across that plate. We need that heat. Heat is good." The words by the squawky voice reminded Peter of the taunting he took as a batter. The taunting that made him lose his focus sometimes.

"I know what you mean. The pitcher Henderson isn't waiting around. Here comes the pitch," said the bored voice.

"Ka-pow. There it goes. Whoa, look at it fly." The squawky voice sounded like he wanted to fly away, too, from his fellow bored announcer.

"Yeah, look at it go. Wow, it's up and up and up and... it's outta here! Sing a song of goodbye." How could the bored announcer sound so bored?

Peter wished he had hit the ball out of the park the last time he was at bat. He held Gabriel close as he remembered the last thing he saw waiting for the pitch. He wished he had kept his eyes on that fast ball instead of the shortstop shifting his position. Peter felt no pain when the ball caught him in his left temple, where he didn't even have eyes. He remembered this despite trying to forget.

To get away from the baseball game, Peter walked toward voices asking for names and addresses. He wanted his name announced. Yet, he smelled the train woman nearby.

"Which direction are you?" Peter called out.

"How did you know I was here?"

"Gabriel told me."

"That's a smart teddy bear. I'm to your left, four steps."

"I would have followed you off the train, but it kept moving." Peter took an extra step and bumped into the woman. He felt her breasts punch back.

"I didn't mean to tell you so much about my problem. You see, this cancer I have is my fault. I was ugly to people who loved me. I got sick as a result."

The woman's regret flooded Peter, who held Gabriel away from the onslaught of words. They stood in a lobby of the wandering public who had their own problems to not listen to.

As her panting, fear-bathed breath enveloped him, Peter said, "I worry that my blindness was my fault, too. I rejected people's kindness and love, even after I got blind." He resented what he had become, holding a teddy bear as his only friend.

A din of noise from the lobby hurt Peter's hearing. The room's mix of colognes, perfumes, and raw sweat cancelled out his smelling sense. He had no seeing sense. He licked his dry lips and tasted nothing. Peter reached out and felt the woman's hand touch his, stopping his approach.

"Both of us are no good at making friends," she said.

He held her hand firmly, afraid she would slip away again. "I got Gabriel 'cause I needed a friend 'cause I'm not good at friends. Gabriel is my angel. But I could use a human friend, too," said Peter.

"I need someone to make me feel less alone. Maybe I should get a teddy bear, too."

At that moment, Peter understood friends and a feeling of calmness stayed with him. "You're like a storm approaching. A gorgeous excitement. I want to help you."

"You don't know the real me to help," she said.

"Tell me."

"When I was young, my dad killed my mom in a drunken rage and he died in a prison fight. I lived with my grandparents, who lived long enough to help me graduate high school. Instead of college, I did drugs with artificial friends, converted to alcohol 'cause the drugs were unpredictable. I was ugly to everybody and no one stuck around when the cancer found me. Where's your family?"

"I was the only child of loving parents. To compensate, I grew an ego so I could love baseball more than I could love them." Peter held Gabriel a little closer. "I was a shit for a son and I think my blindness is my punishment."

"You know what you got with your blindness," she said. "But I don't know how much pain I got comin' to me. I'm going to face medical torture. I wanted a baby growin' in me. 'Stead, I got dead stuff eatin' me up."

She created silence between them as people made noise around their bodies. Finally, she said, "I don't know, sure why not if you want to help. I'm Mary. My cancer 'ppointment's soon. Come on, let's go." She held Peter's hand and led him outside.

They stood on a sidewalk in the hot sun where people brushed by, hurrying away from or toward their destinies. Mary said, "I think everyone knows when it's their time to die and I feel that way now. I'm not going to survive and I don't want to do it alone."

Peter held Gabriel in his arms like cradling a baby, wishing he could see more than gray, fuzzy images around him. He wished this a lot, but he could tell no one. Except maybe Mary.

He reached out and put Gabriel in Mary's hands. "He will be a friend on your cancer journey. Everything is gorgeous when you hug him."

"I can't take your friend."

"It's okay. He wants to help. But I want your kisses along the way. They're gorgeous."

The Performance

I once wrote a one-act play and entered it in a local contest. It won first prize and was performed on stage. It was one of the best moments of my writing life.

Roy shuffled up to the heavy wooden door and dragged it open as his wife, Karen, caught up to him. Inside the theater, they held hands and walked past vacant theater seats to a set of side stairs leading onto the stage.

"Do you remember when we were here back in high school?" Roy walked to the edge of the wide stage where he faced the empty seats. He stood there taking in the grand, ornate expanse of the old theater. Overhead, the high ceilings looked down on him like some celestial hand waiting for the next act.

"This is where we first met. Where our lives began together," Karen said. She moved cautiously toward Roy.

He turned and offered his outstretched hand to his wife. As their fingers touched, the stage lights popped on, dowsing them with brightness.

Smiling, Roy led Karen by the hand to the rear of the stage where their pallid figures blended behind heavy musty curtains, long and massive. They quickly reappeared, tugging and pulling a wide storage trunk out to the center of the stage.

"This is an impressive assortment of costumes," Roy said, pulling the trunk lid open.

"What are we going to do with all of this?" Karen's short, slender figure was frail and the path to this theater had taken a good part of her strength.

"We're putting on a performance. Ta-da!" Roy flopped on a large, green felt hat with an oversized yellow feather drifting off to the side.

"I like this, but where's our script?"

"Just keep remembering and you'll know it. I'll start." Roy kicked off his shoes, slipped on oversized sky-blue socks, a dark red shirt over his own, and walked to the edge of the stage.

In front of the empty theater seats, he threw his head back and raised his arms high over his head in a kind-of salute. The high ceiling of spirals, twists, and circles etched in the plaster became his audience.

Waving his arms in grand fashion over his head, Roy said, "Picture fireworks bursting in a clear night sky. Two young people lean against the hood of a sedan. They smile at the sparkling, exploding colors. Later, they explode within each other in the back seat. From these beginnings, I am born into this world. My chest of red is for the lifeblood that flows in my heart and through my newly born body."

Roy returned to the trunk, leaving his deep voice to echo through the theater and search the empty seats for an ear to hear them.

Karen slipped on a large blue dress over her clothes and tossed off her shoes. She stood in bare feet in the middle of the stage, faced the empty seats, and proclaimed, "I arose from a pint of tequila between two people with too much passion on a hot desert night. I am born a blue baby with no breath to breathe, but of strong will to survive. And I do. I become a dancer among the poverty that greets me." Across the stage, she leaped, hopped, and did a few spirals that terribly impressed Roy.

He kept what he had on and stepped into bulky pink pants before running toward the end of the stage. Karen gasped, thinking he would run away. But Roy dropped to his knees and skidded easily to the edge with his arms outstretched as if to catch an audience applause.

"I arrive to travel through the courts and judgments of the world, reaching the frontier of adulthood. Swiftly, in the most royal of courts, male adolescence adores the goddesses of beauty and fame."

"But, it's a court of questionable appeals." Karen returned to the trunks, dropping the dress and wrapping an emerald green sash around her neck and head. She put on a clown's red nose and wrapped her body in a bright, multi-colored blanket.

Strutting to the front of the stage, she swung her hips from side to side announcing, "The girls of adoration are wild with emotion, as wild as hemlock poison flowing in ancient Rome. All male philosophers beware of the great female presence—youthful talkers in their adolescence rage."

Roy went back to the trunk and returned to the front of the stage with a purple cape flowing behind him. On his head, he balanced a black derby. "A wish for protection as macho stamina meets alluring romance. The manly philosophers search for vitality while the great feminine speakers talk of sentimental drifts."

"Which effect comes first—love or the relationship? A fluttering romantic heart breaks, repairs itself, and starts again in a revolution of many sorts. That is until one soul mate is found at last," Karen said before going back to the trunks.

"Amid the youthful revolution comes a rite of passage and tingling anticipation. Direction is wanted in this new and strange world of adulthood," Roy exclaimed to his imaginary audience.

"Wait!" Karen shouted as she held up a doll the size of a small baby. "Excitement brings a child and partners for life. Is this child safe in this world of sensation? What dreams can she reach? What parental regrets can she make into accomplishments?"

Karen tossed the doll high into the air, where Roy caught the toy infant with both hands. He secured it against his chest.

He tied the cape on the doll. "Look, the child grows with strength and bravery."

"Hopefully. Can she survive under that pressure?" Karen said. She took off what she had and pulled on a puffy-sleeved, lavender blouse before slipping into black high heels. Precariously, she tiptoed about the stage with arms outstretched for balance. "To work go the baby's parents."

Carefully wrapping the doll in the cape for protection, Roy placed it in the trunk on top of discarded costumes. Rummaging around, he found the Greek masks of sadness and happiness.

"Responsibility drives the orb that is our lives," he said, switching the masks back and forth across his face. "I search for purpose as I seek the positive and avoid the negative in this sullen world of respite and work. Is there such a thing as success and failure? Or, just days becoming more days, nights that are the nights. We collect life events as if they are tokens for the trip to another age."

"As I gradually became what I became, I try to learn from mistakes of mine and others," Karen said, returning to the trunks. She threw off her dress and heels and put on a heavy brown coat. A wide brim hat hid part of her face as her silver hair circled her chin. "And the child grows and, yes, she becomes what she is to become through our fault or not. Is it destiny? Is it fate? Is it her decision or ours? It does not matter as long as she is the happiest."

Roy put down the masks and threw off his costumes. On his head, he adjusted a wig with long, curly dark fibers. The wig remained crooked and the dark hair hid parts of his face.

Karen giggled as she faced him on the opposite side of the trunk. She looked cosmopolitan in her hat, dapperly cocked to the side in Bergman style. "What must we fit into the next stage of living? The search for happiness has succumbed to a search for uniqueness and continuance."

"We must look for experience to paint ourselves with color."

"What a crock. I've had my fill of experience and I look for a continuation of my happiness," she said with hands on hips and a wry smile.

They looked at each other for a moment, then dashed wildly into the costumes, strewing them haphazardly across the stage floor.

Karen held a blue chiffon dress before her that flared out to the stage floor. It looked like dry, antiquated paper in her hands. She slipped on yellow rimmed, round eyeglasses that covered half her face. "The child is grown, our task finished. We face each other too much."

"But I'm right here with you. We're in love again." Roy held a bow tie to his neck while wearing black rimmed glasses with a bold, dark bushy, all too fake, of a mustache.

"No, I'm afraid you die," Karen said matter-of-factly, letting drop what pieces of costume she held in her frail hands. They fluttered to her feet. "And I've got to dispose of your body and confront your photographs."

"That's the nature of things." Roy placed his clothing thoughtfully into the trunk. "The arrows of time and the tendrils of age decay physical form. Death comes in this clockwork universe."

They held hands and walked slowly to the edge of the stage. There, they sat dangling their legs over the rim like children. Unexpectedly, they felt exhausted.

"I came to this place, away from the silence of my death. I'm glad you were here to meet me," Karen said.

"I met you here, beyond the final gasp of breath and the last thump of a heart. The high school stage where we first met and from where we will exit together."

As the theater filled with mortal people, young and ambitious, Roy and Karen slipped off the edge of the stage. They sent cold chills through lives yet to be completed.

About the Author

Thank you for reading my short stories.

I grew up on a dairy farm in Spotsylvania, Virginia and ended up commuting to the Pentagon from south Stafford County. To keep my sanity over the commute and politics, I wrote over fifty short stories. More than two dozen were published by magazines and journals.

I escaped the long commute and politics and moved to New Bern, North Carolina (a place I had never been to before). Here, along with volunteer work, I write novels. Yet, I still like reading and writing short stories.

I hope you enjoyed *A Chance to Tell Ten Stories.*

My website is https://stanleybtrice.com/

www.ingramcontent.com/pod-product-compliance
Lightning Source LLC
Chambersburg PA
CBHW021703110726
47902CB00007B/2045